D1201133

The Uncharted Heart

the Uncharted HeaRt

MELISSA HARDY

ALFRED A. KNOPF CANADA

For my husband, Ken Trevenna, with love and thanks always

PUBLISHED BY ALFRED A. KNOPF CANADA

Copyright © 2001 by Melissa Hardy

All rights reserved under International and Pan-American Copyright Conventions.
Published in 2001 by Alfred A. Knopf Canada, a division of
Random House of Canada Limited, Toronto.
Distributed by Random House of Canada Limited, Toronto.

Knopf Canada and colophon are trademarks.

Canadian Cataloguing in Publication Data

Hardy, Melissa
The uncharted heart

ISBN 0-676-97343-4

I. Title.

PS8565.A63243U52 2001   C813'.54   C00-933213-8
PR9199.3.H37U52 2001

First Edition

Visit Random House of Canada Limited's Web site: www.randomhouse.ca

Printed and bound in the United States of America

2 4 6 8 9 7 5 3 1

CONTENTS

LIGHTNING

Bertrand Lanthier had no desire to become such a man as his father, Old Farmer Lanthier — for so Alphonse Lanthier had been known in and about the township of Cobalt since the Quebecer had first come to these parts, as a young man in his thirties. Even then, Old Farmer Lanthier had been possessed of a certain hoary quality: white-haired before his time and grizzly-bearded, with a scratchy voice that rasped like a rusty file and a bandy-legged gait. Despite his apparent years, Bertrand's terrible father was a hearty man, barrel-chested, with a nose like a pointed, flared strawberry, flaming cheeks and eyes the blue of gun-metal that did not twinkle so much as they glittered.

"Not sick a day in his life!" his mother declared acrimoniously. She could not say the same for herself. In addition to being called to childbed nine times (which would make anybody sick), she had survived both the black diphtheria and typhoid fever in her youth, and so entertained a lively sense of her own mortality. Not so Old Farmer Lanthier. "He thinks he can get away with anything," she told her son when he complained of his father's evil ways. "It's why he's the schemer and the scamp he is."

For Alphonse measured success in frauds perpetrated and hoaxes gone undetected long enough for him to realize a profit. Lying, swindling, promising what he could not deliver . . . that was Old Farmer Lanthier's *modus operandi*.

"But what does God expect?" he countered when his wife objected to his business methods. "We come to this place because there is such good land here. So says the government. Good land? Rocks and esker! Pebbles. What does it grow? Withered potatoes. Carrots as hairy and crooked as your grandmother's nose. Do you remember your grandmother's nose, Louise? We have almost as many children to feed as I have fingers. Besides, where's the fun in it?"

Everyone agreed that perhaps the worst thing Old Farmer Lanthier ever did was to sell a donkey to a Mrs. Maude Glover, a would-be woman prospector who had come north from New York City to look for gold in the Porcupine region after her baker husband had taken to his bed with the galloping disease.

"I fear my poor Gil has not many months left to live," she explained tearfully to the Lanthiers, dabbing at her red eyes with a linen handkerchief, "and then it is I who must provide for our four little daughters, all under the age of seven and left in the care of my dear sister Jenny for the present."

In the first place, Old Farmer Lanthier should not have encouraged Mrs. Glover in such a foolhardy quest as she had outlined, for it was apparent to all who beheld the fragile, highly strung woman that she would not survive a night in the bush. In the second place, he should have sold her a donkey that was still alive. For the donkey he sold Mrs. Glover was stuffed, moth-eaten, in fact, with unconvincing (being pea green) glass marbles for eyes and mouldy straw leaking out the seams in its sides. Lanthier had bought him for a pittance off an amateur taxidermist who needed more room in his barn, and then sold him to Mrs. Glover for the tidy sum of twenty dollars.

The woman did not awaken to the true condition of the donkey until well after Lanthier had ferried her across the river and left her alone with it on the road to the Porcupine. For more than an hour she urged it forward, first with slices of apple and sticks of carrots, and finally with willow whips, until Billy Big Blood, an old Ojibwa scout, happened down the road.

"That donkey," he advised the woman, "has been dead a considerable time."

"Mark my words," Louise Lanthier warned her husband. "God will strike you dead!"

Farmer Lanthier only laughed. "He has already tried," he informed his wife. "He missed."

He was referring to an incident that had taken place when he was six years old; there he had been, playing at soldiers with pieces of tin on the floor of his bedroom, when lightning struck the family farmhouse outside the little town of Ste.-Agathe-des-Monts and electrocuted his little sister, who lay sleeping in the iron bedstead not three feet away. Subsequently, his sister's bones, suffused with the energy of Heaven as they had been, were believed to have effected several cures of paralytics, and the four-year-old enjoyed a posthumous reputation as a kind of minor local saint: the Blessed Jeanette Lanthier. As for Alphonse, he had suffered not a jolt, although he did recall the hair on his head and the back of his neck standing on end.

Like his mother, Louise, Betrand was a serious person, dark and small. Rectitude flowed through him like sap, sticky and thick, making him vibrant but slow. "A real thinker," Louise observed of her son. However, Bertrand did not think so much as brood or, if his mood should be a lighter one, mull. That is to say, he didn't think in any organized fashion — logically, with one thought following on the heels of another like soldiers of a regiment. Instead, notions scudded through his mind like loose, vapoury clouds driven across a bright sky by a brisk wind, or else they blew up like storms, crashing into one another and precipitating cogitative crises:

All was not right. There was something vaguely wrong. He couldn't put his finger on just what it might be.

His father was a wicked man. His mother, on the other hand, was a saint.

He did not want to be a farmer.

Should he shoot himself with his father's double-barrelled shotgun? Perhaps not.

May the Blessed Jeanette preserve him against the toils and snares of his outrageous father!

He could run away.

Where?

That girl, Josephine, down the next concession. How would she feel when she heard he had shot himself? Would she be sorry? Would she light a candle for him in the church? Did she know he existed?

These were the sort of things Bertrand thought about: lightning, hail and thunder.

To get away from his father, Betrand signed up with Frères Rancourt the winter he was seventeen. Frères Rancourt, or F.R., as it was referred to, was a lumber camp working the bush country north of Cobalt and almost due west of Timmins, in and around the Thornloe district and the Kenogamissi Lake system. Old Farmer Lanthier would not let the boy go in the spring or the summer, when it took all hands to put the crops into the ground and, later, to take them out. But Bertrand was free to go in the winter; after all, this was Old Farmer Lanthier's time to sit in front of the fire concocting new scams and fresh plots, as well as being the time lumber camps were most active — in the summer, the majority of loggers turned farmer or worked until the first freeze as sawyers in the mills provided by the camps.

"Go! Enjoy!" Lanthier encouraged his son. Despite Bertrand's palpable hostility towards him, Old Farmer Lanthier never failed to display a generous affection towards his first-born; he seemed not to notice his scowls and dirty looks. "Lots to eat in a lumber camp, and more for us here too! Beans! Flapjacks! You will learn many fine songs, which you can teach to me when you return, songs like 'The Jam on Jerry's Rock'." And Lanthier proceeded to rasp in his croaky voice, "You shantyboys, you drivers, come list while I relate / concerning a young riverman and his untimely fate. . . ."

Lumbering was big business in the north wood. With the opening up of the mines in Timmins and Cobalt and Kirkland Lake, there were headframes to be raised and mill-holes to be timbered so the ore could be passed to the surface. There were frames for the tarpaper-covered Hollinger houses (which must be thrown up before this winter or the next) and swale roads to be corduroyed with tamarack (so they would be passable in the spring) and ties for railway tracks.

Bertrand liked living in the F.R. camp. He like the low log shanty, which consisted of sixteen bunks crowded around a big *cambuse* fire. Since the camp moved from logging season to logging season — its location dependent on the availability of good timber and a stand of, preferably, good white pine along a river to float the logs down — the shanty was a temporary structure, thrown up over the course of a day or two and, of necessity, simple in design, with only one door and no windows or hearth, but just the *cambuse* fire at its centre, with a hole cut overhead to let out the smoke.

Lying on his bunk (called a muzzleloader because it was so narrow a man had to crawl into it from the end on his hands and knees), Bertrand could see the stars and the moon of a night while remaining right snug on account of the thick Hudson's Bay blanket (which came with the straw tick on the bunk) and the *cambuse* fire. This was never allowed to go out, for not only did it heat the shanty, but all the loggers' meals were cooked on it as well: oatmeal; prunes; pork and beans, or salt pork cut in pieces and rolled in brown sugar, then fried; bread; butter and cheese for their 5 a.m. breakfast. And then, at 7 p.m., Cook would go outside the shanty and blow on his trumpet to call the men in from the woods for supper: pea soup, beef, pork and mustard, sugar pie, raisin pie and molasses cookies, all washed down with gallons of sweet, steaming tea and everything either boiled in a pot or else baked on shovels pushed into the mound of hot sand on which the logs and kindling were piled to keep the slivery floor from catching fire. Lunch they assembled for themselves out of the bread, cheese and pork that Cook set out on a trestle table just outside the shanty door, and they took it to the woods with them in a tin bucket.

Cook was a large and fussy man, frequently given to loud remonstrances of despair and ennui. He wore a bowler hat to cover his bald spot. Cook wouldn't stand for complaints about his food — "I become *fou!*" he threatened. "*Complement fou!*" Consequently, the men were forbidden to talk during meals. Instead, they crawled into the bunks with their heavily laden tin plates (there being no table inside the shanty) and ate their supper in silence. The only utensils they used were hunting knives and big wooden spoons for soup. When each man was done eating, he stuck his knife in the wall beside his bunk until the next meal. Bertrand didn't mind not talking at meals, because in addition to curbing complaints about the food, it cut down on the number of fights that erupted among the loggers, and after a day in the forest, he was too weary to fight or put up with others fighting in such close quarters.

Everyone had a job to do at the logging camp. Cruisers scoured the forest for the best stands of timber, preferably white pine, which is strong and yields more planks per log than other sorts of trees — F.R. was paid a premium for white pine by sawyers. Fallers cut down trees in teams of two, working in tandem: one faller picked the tree's lay, then he chopped the guiding undercut while his partner sawed the overcut. When the cuts met, the tree toppled over to cries of "Timber-r-r-r!" Buckers then sawed the logs into shorter lengths for the big Clydesdales to drag from the bush, while also burning the camp's initials, F.R., into the dark heartwood of the cut end with a brand (loggers were paid by the piece, and this way an accurate count could be made when the logs reached the millpond downstream). Then they limbed the logs clean, sometimes peeling them of bark for ease of skidding. After that, the skidders hauled the logs to the river on big horse-drawn sleighs called go-devils, which were piled sometimes three storeys high with timber. Finally, river drivers pushed the jumbled logs downstream from the rollaway and kept them moving to the mill, breaking up jams as they occurred with cant hooks or, if that failed, charges of dynamite.

All this work was overseen by Roald Rancourt, one of the seven Rancourt brothers, a burley six-footer with massive shoulders and an equally massive belly. His face appeared buried in an explosion of fierce red beard: all that was visible were two sharp eyes the colour of bright moss and the rounded tip of an absurdly small, pink nose. The loggers called Roald the Bull of the Woods, and greatly admired the man for his skill, knowledge and strength.

"The Bull of the Woods is so tough that bears permit him to ride on their backs," Marcel Dubois confided in Bertrand. Marcel occupied the bunk directly above Bertrand's.

"He can kick so high when he dances a jig that he leaves footprints in the soot on the ceiling," added Paul Gauthier, who slept one bunk over.

The Bull of the Woods was so secure in his manhood and so cognizant of the high repute in which he was held by others that on Sunday nights, he would tie an empty flour sack around his waist to simulate a skirt and a handkerchief to his arm to suggest a frilly sleeve and assume the part of a big red-haired woman in the loggers' jigs and reels across the cornstarch-strewn shanty floor, kicking up his heels in a coquettish manner, his hands on his hips, and tossing his head like a young girl who knows all eyes are on her.

The Bull of the Woods knew everyone's job, and a few more besides. He was the camp's physician, for example, and could set an arm or sew up a wound like a real doctor, for among the farmers who logged during the winter months to make a few extra dollars, there was always someone cutting himself with an axe or getting a hand blown off setting a dynamite charge.

One afternoon in late March, a freak thunderstorm blew up. The ice was still thick on the Kenogamissi and the snow had barely begun to shrink; no one expected thunder and lightning this early in the season. But boiling in from the northwest came the big, brawling clouds, every shade of black or grey there is and driven by a wind that smelled of sulphur and tasted green and somewhat metallic. The forest shuddered; tree branches rattled, making a sound like dry bones knocked together — a hollow, sardonic sound, just a little merry.

"Everybody out of the bush! Back to the shanty!" the Bull of the Woods bellowed, and turning to the team of buckers working with him, he directed them to round up those men who were out of earshot. "Corbel, you go north. Doré, head west towards the river. Duprès, east. Dubois, head south. Get them all in. Heaven is putting on a show." And he squinted up at the sky. Spikes of forked lightning tore through the milling, jostling clouds, darting like the quick, fiery tongues of snakes. From somewhere close by came a rumbling sound, vaguely tectonic in nature, as if the earth's molten core had hunched and then shrugged its rocky shoulders.

Bertrand was up a tamarack, cutting off its crown, when the storm blew up. This section of forest was virgin and the stand old growth: the trees were tall and set so close together that there was no place they could fall except up against one another. Therefore, the first several trees to be harvested had to be shortened so that the horses wouldn't have too hard a time pulling them clear. Bertrand sent the crown crashing to the ground with a desultory "Timber-r-r-r!" (since there was no one but him and his partner, Jules Fornier, in the vicinity) and shimmied down the trunk to a sturdy branch about five feet from the ground. Reaching down, he grasped the steadying hand Jules offered him and was just about to jump to the ground when lightning struck him in the back, just between the shoulder blades. The force of the bolt was such that it flung Bertrand out of the tree and hurled him through the air a full ten feet before gravity asserted itself and he plummeted to the ground like a sack of stones.

As for Jules, who had been holding Bertrand's hand at the moment of the strike, the lightning travelled down his left arm, into his armpit, through his groin and out his left leg. He sat down hard on the ground underneath the tamarack tree, his legs extended straight in front of him, his eyes bugging out and his mouth wide open.

The Bull of the Woods — smelling the electricity as well as the unmistakable odour of burnt flesh and singed hair — lumbered into the clearing, nearly trampling on Bertrand, who lay spread-eagled on the ground, apparently dead.

The Bull dropped to his knees beside the supine body. "Lanthier! Lanthier!" he bellowed, grabbing the boy by the shoulders and shaking him vigorously.

At this, Jules pulled his knees up to his chest, laid his right cheek on his kneecaps and pitched rapidly forwards and backwards, moaning.

Pierre Doré, hearing all the commotion, charged into the clearing. "What happened? *Mon Dieu*, Jules! Where are your clothes, man?" For the lightning had burnt all Jules's clothes on the left side of his body and melted his St. Christopher's medal into the flesh of his chest to boot.

"Ack!" replied Jules, leaping to his feet and surveying his body, which, in addition to being half-naked, was covered with third-degree burns. "Yeek! Yeek!" He screamed in horror and began dashing madly about.

"Restrain him, Doré!" the Bull ordered, alternately pounding Bertrand on the chest and blowing into his mouth. "Wrestle him down!"

"But, boss," argued Doré, "surely *le petit* Lanthier is dead. Hadn't we better tend to Jules here?"

"A man who can run around and scream after he's been struck by lightning is a man who will certainly recover," the Bull informed the bucker. "It's the ones who look dead that you have to tend to." And he continued to pummel Bertrand on the chest with his fist and to roll him vigorously this way and that and, pinching the boy's nostrils between his rough fingers and bending over his prone body, to blow his breath into Bertrand's lungs.

In the meantime, Doré chased the hysterical Jules twice around the clearing before forcing him out onto the skid road. Then he chased him all the way through the woods to the shanty, where four brawny teamsters succeeded in wrestling the screeching logger to the ground and holding him there until he agreed to calm down so that Cook could treat his burns with butter and honey and his frizzled soul with generous quaffs of his best applejack.

While Bertrand lay on his back in the clearing, apparently unconscious and in cardiopulmonary arrest as a consequence of having served as a conduit for approximately twenty thousand amps of electricity, there was a part of him (perhaps it could be called his self) that remained not only amazingly alert, but also endowed with a distinctly heightened awareness. It seemed that the lightning's jagged passage had severed this bit from Bertrand's corporeal being, and now it bobbled some ten feet above his prone self, buoyant as a helium balloon, gelatinous in substance, though not quite concealed, and capable of rising farther but still tugged at by a combination of gravity and the sort of morbid curiosity people exhibit at an accident scene. "*Eh bien!*" it clucked, looking down on the limp vessel that had once contained it. "Bertrand is surely done for now! There's no walking away from such a calamity as this!"

No sooner had the chunk of disengaged consciousness observed this than there was the sound of rushing wind, of huge, slowly beating wings, and in the distance, through a break in the dark clouds where blue heaven might be glimpsed, the fluid tinkling of harps. Bertrand's disembodied self watched as a great pink cloud billowed and swelled through this break like some rosy surf. Borne upon it, as though on a litter, was a little girl of about four, with pink cheeks and blonde curls and eyes as blue as the periwinkles that peek through the snow in late May.

"*Bonjour, mon neveu,*" the creature proclaimed in silvery tones. "*Je suis ta tante Jeanette!*"

"*Mais, sainte tante,* you are not fried to a crisp!" Bertrand's self cried out. For according to Old Farmer Lanthier, what was left of his sister after she was struck by lightning resembled a crumbling side of burnt bacon. ("And smelled that way, too," his father used to observe. "Ummm!" To which his mother, wounded by his irreverence, would cry, "*Barbare!*") Bertrand's self hesitated to make the rather indelicate observation that his aunt seemed much prettier than in the one existing photograph of her, taken by an itinerant photographer who prophetically observed that were anything ever to happen to Jeanette, her mother would not take two dollars for it: the dog-eared print, smeared with the kisses of the pious, portrayed her as a thin-faced child with lank, dark hair and a rather sallow complexion.

Jeanette must have read his confusion in his reticence. "Ah, but you see," she said, "this is my resurrected body! Do you like it?" And she extended a plump, pink hand to Bertrand. As she did, the gap in the clouds widened perceptibly, yawning, and the sound of harps playing became more distinct.

At just that moment, the corporeal Bertrand opened his eyes and found himself locked in the embrace of the Bull of the Woods, their lips sealed in a profound kiss. "Umppph!" he managed, whereupon the Bull of the Woods reared back, wiping his mouth with the back of his hand as he did.

"You're alive?" he demanded.

Bertrand's eyes rolled from side to side, taking in the snow in which he lay, the dark sentinels of tall trees, the black sky, aching with rain. He opened his lips to respond, but the only sound that emerged from them was an eerie creaking.

After being struck by lightning, Bertrand was unfit to work at the lumber camp. Although he recovered the use of his limbs and his vocal cords within a few days of the accident, his motor skills and hand-eye coordination were much impaired. He now walked in a haphazard, flopping way, like a clown with oversized, flat shoes, his arms flapping by his sides and his head lolling on his neck. The lightning had sapped him of strength. He was weak, flaccid, prone to migraines and sudden neurological storms — and during these attacks, he was subject to spasms of the eyeball, uncontrollable finger flicking and violent twitches. He suffered from a sensation of pins and needles in his feet, hands and backside; his body ached like a tooth; and he forgot the oddest things, like where the outhouse was.

Old Farmer Lanthier shook his head. "Looks like God missed again," he observed. "Hee! Hee!"

"Alphonse!" Bertrand's mother warned him. Picking up a cast-iron skillet by the handle, she waved it menacingly at her husband.

"All right. You are right, Louise," Alphonse conceded. "It's a terrible thing that happened to Bert. But we must think about what to do with the boy. He's no good for farm work now."

"He can slop hogs," Louise pointed out.

"That is correct. Pigs and chickens are not particular," admitted Alphonse. "But neither is God. Why doesn't our Bertie become a priest?"

"A priest!" Louise repeated with a mixture of disbelief and scorn. "Can I be hearing this from the greatest scoundrel on the planet?"

Old Farmer Lanthier shrugged modestly. "Surely not the greatest," he demurred. "But think of it: If Bertie entered orders, he would have a roof over his head and there would be more food on the table for everybody (that is, except the priests), for if there's one thing I've noticed, it's that being struck by lightning has not interfered with our son's appetite."

"A priest!" Louise entoned, rapturous.

Bertrand was changed in other ways by his accident. For example, he no longer dreamed of Josephine down the road, but now dreamed of Roald Rancourt, whose kiss had restored him to life. He thought of the Bull of the Woods day and night: of the strong hands that had so urgently gripped his shoulders and shaken him like one of his sisters' string dolls; of the massive arms that had cradled him and borne him up in them as effortlessly as if he had been a baby; of the heady, profound way the overseer smelled of fresh, cold air and woodsmoke and the clean, pine woods ... and in other ways, too, which he was certain were not quite pure. At length, he hissed his secret to Father Joseph in the ramshackle confessional of St. Mary's in Cobalt.

"Do not trouble yourself, my son," Father Joseph rumbled back through the fly-blown grating. "I myself have never found women attractive. It is my understanding — correct me if I am wrong — that they leak. Well, you would know about that, having sisters. Such substances as I've never — humph! — cared to inquire about."

The priest cleared his throat. Louise had spoken to him of Bertrand. Meanwhile, the bishop, desperately short of labour in these remote northern regions, had established only one criterion for a man's acceptance into the priesthood: "Pants!"

"Perhaps you have a vocation ... ?" Father Joseph dangled the idea before the young lightning victim as though it were a particularly fat worm on a particularly shiny hook. "Hmm? Hmm?" Waggle, waggle.

But Bertrand did not absorb new concepts readily. The notion beaded on him like water on an oiled surface, wobbling there before sliding off. He was not yet ready to embrace the God who had struck him down in his prime, so, taking his hat, he careered down the church's aisle, his flat feet making a slapping noise against the worn red carpet. Inside his skull a storm was brewing: dark clouds, wind, rain and bright spikes of cruel lightning.

In late August, Old Farmer Lanthier's grandmother, Maman Lanthier, died, full of years. Indeed, at the time of her death, she was the oldest woman in the diocese of Ste.-Agathe-des-Monts, having wrung a full 103 years from what must have been an extremely hearty constitution. Her death did not distress Old Farmer Lanthier overmuch; after all, he had left home at twenty and had received only sporadic word from his family in the intervening three decades. Now, however, he was determined to pay a visit to the town of his birth.

"But the harvest will be in any day now," Louise objected.

"So why did we have so many sons?" Old Lanthier countered. "Four when I last counted. Let them bring in the harvest this year. Maman has left the clothes press to me, and if I don't go and fetch it right away, my brother Pierre will steal it from me."

The clothes press was a legendary piece of furniture, as large as a small room and made of white pine, with painted panels. It had been in the Lanthier family for two hundred years, and its disposition had been the subject of much heated debate from Maman's sixtieth birthday (when it was assumed that her death would be imminent) onward. Finally, Maman had settled the matter by willing the clothes press to the oldest surviving Lanthier son, Alphonse, with the stipulation that should he not come from Northern Ontario to fetch it within the specified time period of two months, ownership of the armoire would revert to Pierre, the second oldest. Already a month had passed when Alphonse received the letter informing him of Maman's death, Pierre having forgotten to mail it for several weeks, "owing to a little problem I've been having with my memory."

"Memory, the hole in my behind!" Old Farmer Lanthier expostulated.

"Well, if you are going off to Ste.-Agathe-des-Monts, then I'm going too," said Louise, eager to see old friends.

Alphonse and Louise rented two big dray horses and a ramshackle wagon from the tanner in Cobalt, and headed south and east into Quebec. Three weeks later, they returned with a clothes press as big as the wagon bed and a full seven feet high; it was swaddled in old blankets like a huge, square baby and required five men to carry it from the wagon into the house, where it took up a full third of the sitting room.

"This will never do!" Louise objected. "The house was too small to begin with. Now there's no room for us!"

"Quiet!" Old Farmer Lanthier ordered her. "You will see! I shall build a special room for it one of these days."

The clothes press wasn't all the Lanthiers had brought back.

"Hee! Hee! Stold it right from under Pierre's big nose!" Old Farmer Lanthier explained to Bertrand. "It was in the press all the time, but can you believe it? I didn't think to mention it to him. No, nor to your tante Elise either! A little problem with my memory. . . ." He held in his hands some kind of box wrapped in fragments of an old quilt and tied with string. It was about three feet long and eighteen inches wide.

"What is it?" Bertrand asked.

His father handed it to him. "Go ahead. Unwrap it," he encouraged his son.

Bertrand set the box on the table, cut the twine with his pocket knife, then pulled back the quilt to reveal a crystal casket with gilded fittings. In the casket were the jumbled bones and slightly blackened skull of a small child. Bits of rotted cloth clung to the bones, and clotted dust that might have once been hair to the skull.

"Tah! Dah!" Alphonse crowed, clapping his hands. "Your blessed tante Jeanette!"

"But, why . . . ?" Bertrand was confused. "Wasn't she buried in the churchyard?"

"She was! Ah, but everyone wanted to know: Would she decompose?"

"Saints don't decompose," his mother interjected.

"Ehh!" Old Farmer Lanthier made an equivocating gesture with his hand. "Some do, some don't. It depends on the soil they're buried in. Why, I know of a very fat woman who turned entirely to soap, and no one could have called Marie-Paule Benoît a saint! Not with the mouth on her!"

"Well, I can tell you this much: St. Bernadette of Lourdes didn't decompose!" Louise argued.

"She turned black!" her husband countered.

"That's another matter altogether!" Louise declared, her feathers somewhat ruffled. She turned to Bertrand. "I have a special devotion to the little shepherdess," she explained. "When I was but a small child, our pastor went on a pilgrimage to Lourdes. The holy water he brought back cured my granny's blindness. I shall never forget the moment when she rubbed her old eyes, then blinked and laughed and flung her cane to one side, crying, 'Saints in Heaven, I can see!'"

"Never well, of course," Old Farmer Lanthier observed. "She was forever walking into walls and mistaking the livestock for relations. . . . The point is that following Jeanette's death, her bones did effect quite a number of cures in our little parish of Ste.-Agathe-des-Monts."

At this, Louise nodded earnestly. "It's true," she said. "The only difficulty was that the persons cured died shortly afterwards. Such a shame!"

"Without living witnesses, it is difficult to prove beatitude," said Old Farmer Lanthier.

"Beatitude?" Bertrand wanted to know.

"First you're a blessed, then you're a saint," Louise said, outlining the process. "The Holy Father himself mucks in —"

Farmer Lanthier interrupted her. "Jeanette was in the running for a blessed when she was exhumed and put in this ossuary. But then . . ." The old man shrugged. "No cures."

"Nothing," Louise confirmed. "So disappointing. Not to mention embarrassing. The ossuary remained in the church for a few years. Afterwards, the priest returned it to your father's family. 'Here,' he said. 'This is of no use to us. Do with her what you will.'"

"Jeanette was a dud," Alphonse concluded.

"So she wasn't reburied? She was hidden away in the clothes press instead?" Bertrand asked.

"Such a nice casket! Real crystal. You wouldn't want to bury it!" Louise countered.

"So what do you propose to do with it now?" Bertrand asked.

His father flung his heavy arm around the young man's shoulders. "Well, Bertie, my son, when a man gets to be as old as I am, he begins to think of the Almighty and of the life beyond this one, and the thoughts aren't all pleasant ones, my boy. More like a gallbladder attack. And at the same time, a man my age has responsibilities, obligations, dependent children, cows and chickens and pigs that look to him for sustenance — and that despite the fact that his farm is a poor one, all rocks and roots and sandy esker. So I thought, What if we set up a little shrine to the Blessed Jeanette out by the concession road and tell everyone we know about the cures her bones wrought back in Ste.-Agathe-des-Monts. I tell you, people will come from far and wide to light a candle at her shrine for the sake of a mother's cancer or a baby's crippled legs or cleft palate. The collection box alone will turn a profit, and if the thing takes off, we could establish a hostel for pilgrims. You, Bertie, you could be the sacristan! What do you think about that?"

But Bertrand did not know what to think.

Old Farmer Lanthier was as good as his word. On the side of the muddy corduroy road that led into Cobalt, he built a log chapel just large enough to accommodate the clothes press, a couple of rough benches hewn from logs and a small table on which he set a brass candelabrum, a box of votive candles and a pink china piggy bank. The piggy bank was for offerings. Nailed to the roof's peak was a three-foot cross, and in front of the chapel was a sign that read, in English and French, "See the Saint. Get blessed!"

Alphonse appointed Bertrand sacristan of the chapel. "It's your job to tell pilgrims the story of the Blessed Jeanette. Describe her many amazing miracles. Tell them how she appeared to you in a vision and told you to bring her body to Northern Ontario so that she could confer her blessings on a less stiff-necked people than the French of Ste.-Agathe-des-Monts. Get their money, then let them see the ossuary and light a candle if they wish."

Old Farmer Lanthier hung a cowbell next to the chapel door with a sign. "Ring for service," the sign read.

Bertrand couldn't keep Jeanette's miracles straight. There was someone crippled who walked, throwing away his crutches before tripping over a root on the way home and shattering his kneecap. Another whose pinkeye was cured. Yet another, whom everyone had considered quite mad, who came to seem only peculiar and rather simple in time. On good days, when his brain did not lie limp and ragged within his skull like something a cart wheel thumps over in the road, the former logger made up miracles, with Jeanette curing an entire orphanage of dropsy and, to top it off, restoring to life the children's dead parents, or gluing the head of a Jesuit decapitated by savage Hurons back on his body using miracle spittle. On bad days, he only muttered and said things like "Do you want to see the blessed bones or not?"

Traffic at the shrine was not what Old Farmer Lanthier had hoped for. After an initial flurry of visitors, most of whom were young boys profoundly interested in skeletons of all sorts, the chapel fell into disuse. It was rare that Bertrand had to light the little Quebec heater in the corner, which was a good thing, given that it let fly sparks and, in any case, was placed too close to the log walls not to be a fire hazard.

One year after the chapel was erected, almost two years to the day of Bertrand's accident, lightning struck the cross on its roof and the entire structure, clothes press and all, burned to the ground in the middle of the night. The skeleton of Jeanette survived the flames, but the heat of the fire had melted the crystal ossuary around the bones, with the result that they were completely encased and fused with the sparkling, if somewhat scorched, glass.

Old Farmer Lanthier was chagrined at the loss of the clothes press and the chapel but delighted to have once again escaped death by lightning.

"Three times! Three times He's missed!" he crowed, clapping his hands.

"Three times lucky," Louise muttered, implying that her husband had better watch his back from now on.

Old Farmer Lanthier sold the glass-encased skeleton of his little sister to the man who owned the sideshow — he was making a shopping trip through the district looking for such marvels as two-headed calves, dancing chickens and boys without limbs.

For the next twenty years, the bones of the all-but-blessed Jeanette Lanthier would be exhibited throughout Ontario, Quebec and Manitoba as the Glass Girl, and the story told to audiences aghast with wonder of how this little Romanian princess had died when a crystal chandelier, alight with a thousand candles, had crashed down upon her head at a formal function, setting her on fire. "The fire was so fierce, ladies and gentlemen, boys and girls, that no one could approach it. Oh! And the screams of the little girl were terrible, making strong men weep, but to no avail," the carny man barked. "And when the flames finally subsided, this was what was left of the little princess."

THE ICE WOMAN

The big thaw began in April. The sun, so distant and pale throughout the long winter, grew round and yellow. Frost eased from the spruce and the tamarack. Tender, fat buds appeared on the willow and the aspen, while the snow cover sank and shrank with loud sighs before disintegrating in the sun. The swollen land sagged loosely at its joints. Boulders rumbled down the hills into low-lying stream beds, and the ice on Frederick House Lake, still close to four feet thick, growled and creaked, then candled and pulled away from the marshy sedge that edged the lake as though repulsed by it. On the lake's eastern shore, the Hudson's Bay Company trading post floated in its half-acre clearing, forlorn and soggy, on a sea of reeking mud, its red, white, green and yellow flag flapping in a wind that smelled cold and of thickly running sap.

When he was convinced he could break ground, Oliphant ventured out of the post. The apprentice was a young man just past twenty, all wrists and ankles and Adam's apple, with hair the bright colour of rust and a patchy complexion. In one hand he carried a pick, in the other a spade: he intended to bury his master on that little promontory overlooking the lake. It was a pretty place; more important, it was only about fifty feet from the cabin and on somewhat higher ground, and therefore less likely to be boggy.

Burying McGillvary took the better part of the sunny, cool morning. The ground was still partially frozen and chunky with rocks. However, the thought of the factor's corpse slowly thawing out beneath the pile of dry salt bellies that weighted it down in the cold room behind the store was a pressing one: for several weeks now, it seemed to Oliphant that the musty smell he associated with the dried apples stored in that place was beginning to acquire a slightly sweet edge; that it would soon turn, like a knife. McGillvary had been dead, after all, two months.

When he had managed to excavate a hole some three and a half feet deep and seven feet long, Oliphant returned to the post for McGillvary, whom he half dragged, half rolled to the gravesite. Inside the shroud, which the apprentice had improvised out of flour sacks, the factor felt loose, oddly spongy. He leaked a smell so like rotten potatoes that Oliphant had to stop and vomit twice on his way up the rise. Once he lost a Wellington to the muck and had to hop back for it.

When he had finally succeeded in poking into the shallow grave those reluctant, stray bits of McGillvary that persisted in sticking out of it, the apprentice filled in the hole and piled rocks on top of it. Weak with relief and dizzy with the effort, Oliphant stood beside the grave for a moment, his black melton in his hands. "Here's hoping there are no chipmunks in Heaven," he told the rock pile. Then he replaced his hat and took up his pick and his spade. "Well, there's the problem of you solved, anyway," he said by way of conclusion.

It was on his way back to the post that he spotted the girl frozen in the block of green ice.

Oliphant was born in the hamlet of Ayr in Strathclyde. This was across the Firth of Clyde from the isle of Arran. Ayr clung to the rocks like a jagged colony of barnacles — precarious, salt-encrusted, slippery with spray. Houses with soggy thatch roofs, sagging barns and imploded lean-tos. From birth to death, the inhabitants felt their ears ring with the sound of waves crashing tumultuously against the black rock shore. The sound curled in their ears like a fat worm and beat slow there, like a strong heart.

Oliphant was different from other men of Ayr. They loved the sea, the rough and tumble of it, the hale-and-hearty murderousness, the stench and thunder, the slow, green rage. Oliphant hated the sea. He dreamed instead of the vast, blank interior of Canada, a place where it was dry-cold and clean and the sea was far away, tucked safely into extreme distance, its terrible voice muffled by the incessant soft falling of white snow.

For this reason, he answered an advertisement placed by the Hudson's Bay Company in the Glasgow newspaper: "Wanted: apprentice factors to be trained and sent to New Ontario." He was old enough for it and at loose ends in Ayr: too overgrown to have much strength in his limbs, but healthy and possessed of an inordinately fine and spidery copperplate hand, very desirable in a keeper of ledgers.

Oliphant was posted to Frederick House Lake, a point of convergence for the fur trade in the Mattagami-Abitibi region of New Ontario. Porcupine Lake, Pearl Lake and Miller Lake lay to the west of the post, Iroquois Falls and Quebec to the east. McGillvary was the factor at the post, a tall, shuffly man with big shoulders and big hands who had been in the North for most of his fifty years, although he maintained from his distant Scottish youth a rumbling, guttural burr. He scarcely seemed to notice Oliphant, but when he did, he appeared depressed at the younger man's continued presence.

The trading post consisted of a two-room cabin made of peeled and squared logs, whitewashed once a season with lime. Tarpaper was nailed down over the roof and firewood piled high on the porch: jack pine seasoned over the summer, poplar for the cookstove and green birch for the little Quebec heater. Out back a lean-to, which could be entered only through the store, served as a cold room. It was stacked high with furs, which started to smell if they were green and so had to be kept as cool as possible. Barrels of apples and burlap sacks of onions, turnips and potatoes were also kept in the cold room, as was the press, used for baling.

The front room served as the store. On one end of the counter stood a brass beam scale on which the factor weighed purchases. Underneath it crowded bulk barrels of white and brown sugar, cornmeal, rice, navy beans, Scotch mints and jelly beans, along with fireproof tins of matches and plug and chewing tobacco and Copenhagen snuff. The post sold medicine — Gin Pills and Tilden's C. Indice Extract — as well as Victor steel traps, nail kegs, rolls of sheet-metal stove-pipe, roof jacks and dampers, hanks of codline for lashing toboggans, and heavy bolts of Magog and galaplaid. Rubber moccasins and retinned pails with bailed handles dangled from the ceiling.

The second, smaller room was where Oliphant and McGillvary slept on feather ticks suspended on rope hammocks lashed to crude wooden frames and covered with Hudson's Bay Company blankets. There was, fashioned out of a wooden packing crate, a small desk on which McGillvary wrote up his ledgers and a table on which a white china wash basin and water pitcher stood. Nailed to the wall above this table was a sheet of tin — this served the two men as a mirror. Under each bed was a white china chamber pot.

At the opposite end of the narrow room was a black cookstove; a corner cabinet stacked precariously with dishes, utensils, pots and pans; a rickety-legged table on which was set a large tin tub for washing up; and a battered pine table covered with a tattered oilcloth, at which they ate their meals. The chipped granite and tin plates were turned upside down to keep the mice, ubiquitous, off the eating side.

McGillvary went missing in late June, just two months after Oliphant joined him at Frederick House Lake. After ten days, during which Oliphant wrote the company asking for direction, Billy Big Blood, one of the Ojibwa who summered at the post, found the factor marooned on little Crow Island in Nighthawk Lake. McGillvary, who had canoed down the Frederick House River to pick blueberries on the island, had neglected to tether the canoe properly, and so it had floated away as he foraged in the bush, leaving him stranded. When Billy found him, McGillvary was naked, swollen to half again his large size from insect bites, scratched all over from stumbling through brambles and deadfall, and stained dark blue about the hands and face with berry juice. His hair, including the iron grey hair on his chest and around his groin, was matted thickly with burrs.

The factor was delirious for a week, incoherent for another fortnight, then despondent. "I dreamed I had died," he told Oliphant wistfully, his rough voice ragged with regret. "I was light as a dandelion clock and blew here and there. Wherever the wind took me."

Later, Billy found the canoe. That was what the big Indian did, after all — he was a finder. The canoe had drifted across to Grassy Point and got stuck in the high, mucky sedge. Billy paddled it back to the post. "You need a canoe," he told Oliphant.

"Carry on without McGillvary if he has gone missing."
The reply wafted back from the company in late summer,
delivered by a trapper heading north to Moosonee. "After
all, it is not the first time."

In the fall, the half-dozen or so Ojibwa families who had
made their camp around the trading post during the summer loaded all their belongings onto dogsleds and headed
north for their traplines and their winter camp up around
Ice Chest Lake, leaving Oliphant alone at the post with
McGillvary.

Oliphant was sorry to see them go. He liked filling his
pockets with jelly beans and then sneaking them to the
children, and one of the old women had taught him the
Red River jig, which he performed so clumsily that it
made all the Ojibwas laugh and clap their hands.

McGillvary, on the other hand, was not such good
company. Since his rescue, he had remained lying on his
bed in the little room he shared with the apprentice, his
face to the wall. Now and then he sighed long and low —
it sounded as though someone were letting the air out of
him. Sometimes he groaned.

Within a week of the Ojibwas' departure, winter arrived.
The blue eye of the lake scummed over with ice. One night

in late October, it stormed. When Oliphant awoke, the lake shone white in the pale sunlight; a membrane of ice coated it like a milky cataract glazes an eye. At first, Oliphant could stand on the dock and make out the silvery glint of fish moving below the surface of the ice; then, as the days and weeks passed and the temperature dropped to minus thirty and forty and the ice thickened to three, four, five feet, the factor's apprentice could no longer see what went on inside the bowl of frigid water. It became a world apart: dark and slow, inhabited by things that floated and slept.

Occasionally the ice would explode with a loud boom. There were other noises too: a crackling sound (like phosphorus makes) when Oliphant filled the battered tea pail, the pop and hiss of cedars and balsams cracked open by the cold. Apart from these sorts of sudden and surprising sounds, however, snow muffled the world and laced it up tight with cold.

The company shipped coal oil to the post, two four-gallon tins to the case for ease of portaging, but only during the summer, when the waterways were clear. In order to conserve their oil, Oliphant went to bed shortly after sunset and arose just after dawn; as for McGillvary, he rarely got out of bed at all. This meant that during December, January and February, the apprentice lay in bed for close to twelve hours a day, listening to McGillvary moan and to the mice — which made their home in the half-inch of space between the room's interior wall of pine tongue-and-groove wainscoting and sooty hessian and the exterior log wall of the post — scurry back and forth, back and forth.

"There must be hundreds of them," observed Oliphant.

"Thousands," McGillvary corrected him through clenched teeth.

"We should get a cat."

"Not a cat within a hundred miles of here," McGillvary pointed out. "The only solution is to burn the place down!"

"No need for that, surely!" Oliphant exclaimed warily. He had no idea what extremes McGillvary, mobilized, might be capable of.

"There are thousands of them and only two of us," McGillvary reminded him. "The racket!" he moaned, tossing lightly. "The infernal racket of their little feet!"

On the second of February, the factor rose from his bed. As he was out of practice, he walked unsteadily, shuffling his feet and having to catch hold of furniture now and again to secure his balance. First, he took an auger from his red metal tool chest and punched holes in a dozen tin plates. Then he threaded ropes through the holes and knotted them at the end, hammered nails into the rafters and suspended the plates from the nails. They hung about six feet above the floor. He removed the bags of flour and cornmeal and oatmeal from the shelves and set them on the plates.

"What did you do that for?" Oliphant asked.

"Let them jump!" McGillvary exclaimed, his face working, his eyes feverish. "Let the little devils jump if they want to eat!" He stumbled back to bed.

In the following days, there was no noticeable diminution of noise coming from between the walls. Indeed, if anything, McGillvary's actions seemed to have emboldened the mice, which started to appear here and there about the cabin in daylight hours — on the table, eating crumbs that Oliphant had neglected to sweep away, skittering like novice skaters across the back of the upturned plates, gnawing at the tattered, rust-stained oilcloth. Accordingly, McGillvary arose from his bed a second time, again took up his auger and bored holes in four more tin plates, which he then forced up the table legs, with the inverted side down. "Now let them get on our table with their dirty feet!" he declared triumphantly and, handing Oliphant the auger, returned to bed.

Three nights later, McGillvary went to use his chamber pot, only to find a mouse staring forlornly up at him.

"That does it!" he advised Oliphant.

Working on McGillvary's instructions, Oliphant set a ten-gallon pail half filled with water under the table and tipped a narrow plank of board against it. Then he drove a nail halfway into the underside of the table and dangled a strip of salt pork from it.

"I thought of this while I was resting," McGillvary told Oliphant. "It's foolproof. The mice run up the plank to get the salt pork, fall into the water and drown."

Each morning for a week, McGillvary made Oliphant inspect the bucket and report on the number of casualties.

"Six," Oliphant would call out.

"Seven!"

One banner morning, there were fourteen.

At first McGillvary was exultant, but after a while he lapsed back into despondency. "What's the point?" he asked. "Even as we pick off the stragglers, they are breeding, multiplying,"

One day Oliphant, who was doing a desultory sort of inventory, made a discovery. "There's a nest of chipmunks behind the bulk barrels," he told McGillvary.

"Chipmunks!" McGillvary sat up in bed. "Chipmunks, did you say?"

"Chipmunks," Oliphant confirmed.

"It's the end," McGillvary informed the apprentice, squeezing his temples between flattened palms. Then, his voice rising in pitch, he shouted, "Chipmunks! They'll eat it all, them and their babies, and what they don't devour, the mice will! There will be nothing left! We'll be stripped bare! They'll eat the very clothes off our bodies! You don't know, Oliphant! You don't understand! We'll starve! We'll freeze!"

"They're very small," Oliphant said uneasily.

But the distracted factor would not be soothed. "Nibble! Nibble! Nibble!" he muttered, wringing his hands as he rocked backwards and forwards on the bed.

So McGillvary arose again from his bed, going so far this time as to wrestle a crumpled Viyella shirt, stiff with stains, over his long johns. He sat himself down at the opposite end of the store with his twenty-two, and every time a chipmunk appeared on the counter or popped up from between the barrels, he shot at it. Soon there were bullet holes in everything.

"Is this a good idea?" Oliphant asked, but the factor only looked at him in a way that suggested that, under the circumstances, the younger man would do well to hold his tongue.

At just past four in the afternoon on March 8, as Oliphant was standing at the pine table, dripping slushy Eagle's Condensed Milk into a mug of Red Rose tea, McGillvary took aim at a chipmunk skittering across the brass beam scale on the counter. The bullet ricocheted off the scale, hitting the factor square in the middle of the forehead. McGillvary pitched backwards and then lay still on the floor. Oliphant turned, and flinging open the door between the rooms, he lunged towards the factor, dropped to his knees and, seizing him by both shoulders, shook him.

"Mr. McGillvary!" he cried.

There was a bright red spot in the middle of the factor's forehead.

"Mr. McGillvary, sir!"

Oliphant laid his ear on McGillvary's chest to listen for a heartbeat. Nothing. He grabbed the factor's wrist and tried to find a pulse there. Again, nothing.

"Mr. McGillvary! Mr. McGillvary!"

Not even a twitch. The factor's mouth was slack, his eyes wide open.

Oliphant sank back onto his haunches. "By gum!" he exclaimed softly. "I believe he's . . . dead!"

The apprentice had seen dead people, of course, back in Ayr — his grandmother, for instance, and a neighbour who toppled off a wagon while drunk and was trampled by dray horses — but others had informed him in advance that they were dead; he hadn't had to figure it out for himself.

Oliphant stood.

It didn't seem right somehow that McGillvary should go so quickly, struck by a bullet intended for a chipmunk. He should have cried out, Oliphant thought, or at the very least, thrashed.

He crossed back to the door and retrieved his cup of tea from the table. It was still hot. "Not much I can do now," he advised McGillvary. "It'll be dark in half an hour. . . ." He took a sip of his tea. "I'll just leave you here overnight . . . you know, in case you revive."

He shut the door between the two rooms. A moment later, upon reflection, he barred it.

The next morning, the factor appeared deader than ever — cold as a rock and the colour of lard. The hole in his forehead had dried to a dark, rusty brown.

"What am I going to do with you?" the apprentice asked McGillvary. "I can't bury you until the ground thaws. I guess I'll put you in the cold room."

He sewed the factor a shroud out of two flour sacks, jammed him into it and rolled him onto a travois he rigged out of a Hudson's Bay blanket and two broom handles lashed together with Gilling twine. Then, to the consternation of the chipmunks, which boiled out of their nest and dashed up and down the counter, chattering and squeaking, he dragged, bumped and squeezed the rickety travois around the counter and through the door into the cold room, where he wedged his former master into the corner behind a wooden tub of corn syrup and a fifty-pound tin of lard. Just in case McGillvary took it upon himself in his deceased state to get up and walk around, Oliphant piled dried salt bellies in jute bags on top of the corpse. As a final precaution, he padlocked the door.

Then he pulled on his coat and went outside to look at the snow-burdened trees and the shining, glassy lake and the blue sky piled high with clouds. The thermometer that hung from a nail beside the door read fifty-four below. It hurt to breathe, as though he were inhaling razor blades; his breath hissed in his ears like an angry weasel. He went back inside. It took a few minutes of crouching by the angry little

Quebec heater for his fingers to warm up enough to write the company that McGillvary was dead and that he, Oliphant, was now officially alone at Frederick House Lake.

Over the week since the thaw had begun, the current had rolled big blocks of green ice down the river, forming a kind of jumbled ice dam where the river fed the lake. Oliphant had watched the blocks accumulate from the porch; they glittered crystalline in the sunlight, the strange colour of a gemstone he had seen once in a jeweller's window in Glasgow. A peridot, the stone was called.

However, it was a fine day — the sun bright and warm, the temperature a degree above freezing and at last McGillvary was in the ground. The apprentice decided to walk up to the river to have a closer look.

It was uneasy going. The jam had backed up the river for two miles or more, causing the water to seep from its banks across the scrubby bush and sedge, where it half-froze into a trembling sheet of ice that bent under Oliphant's weight and sometimes broke through. To his right stretched muskeg — tamarack and black spruce and sphagnum — bottomless, impossible to traverse in the thaw. Instead, the factor's apprentice cut north and around to reach the river's edge, through a stand of cedar and balsam.

The ice wall stood three times his height, and the blocks that composed it were much larger than he had imagined: some were the size of horses, others the size of people. The sun's warmth had caused their surface to melt slightly, making them glisten and sparkle. As the day passed and the sun grew warmer, the ice that bound them together would melt; some of the blocks would slide free and float away, or fall and catch. Then night would come. Once more the temperature would drop, and the remaining blocks would refreeze to form the next day's slightly revised and, as time went on, diminished wall.

Oliphant could make out objects suspended in some of the translucent blocks: the bough of a cedar tree, what looked to be a crumpled mouse, a woman . . .

Oliphant started.

A woman? A woman lying on her side, her knees drawn close to her chest and her long, straight hair floating over her face? That's what it looked like. But no, he told himself. Surely the curved shape was a willow wand or someone's old coat, tangled with marsh grass.

Using his pick to anchor himself on the slick ice, the apprentice climbed up onto the ice jam and crawled over to the block on his hands and knees.

The body was suspended in a frosty cloud that rendered it pale and indistinct — as though the woman had breathed her life out into the water and it had frozen thick about her, forming a kind of hazy cocoon in which she floated. The remainder of the ice block would have formed later, layer upon layer as the winter progressed. Now it was about eighteen inches thick, by Oliphant's reckoning, and as clear and unclouded as glass.

The apprentice lay on his stomach, peering into the chunk.

The curled fingers, not gnarled with age or rough with work, but smooth, seemed those of a younger woman. She was wearing some kind of light-coloured sack dress that came to mid-calf. He remembered how the Ojibwa women had prized coarse flour sacks for such dresses, how they had traded dainty porcupine-quill baskets for them. Over this dress was pulled a jumbo knit sweater with a sailor collar, grey wool, the kind sold at the post. He could just make out the girl's feet through the ice — they were bare and, like her hands, youthful, delicate. Her toes were curled, as though death had been a surprise. He could make out nothing of her face through her black hair.

Oliphant screamed. He didn't know where the scream came from or even that he was frightened before he heard himself howl and felt his eyes strain in his head as though they might pop out onto the ice. Hastily, he crawled backwards off the dam. When he reached the river's marshy shore, he turned and ran, splashing through big puddles to the stand of cedar and balsam. Partridge exploded from the sedge, squawking, and a startled crane lifted out of the long marsh grass, straight up, its legs dangling loosely, as though it were a puppet on strings being hauled away. Oliphant ran all the way to the post, kicked off his Wellingtons on the porch, dashed inside and locked and bolted the door behind him.

"Damnation!" he exploded, clapping his hands together and stomping his frozen feet — the air around the ice dam had been at least fifteen degrees colder than elsewhere. "I thought all I had to do was get McGillvary in the ground, and now there's another one! A woman! A frozen woman! Damnation!"

Reaching under the counter, he retrieved McGillvary's treasured bottle of Scotch malt and poured himself a jigger's worth.

"Of course, it's not that I have to do anything," he reasoned. Not being overused to spirits, he sipped McGillvary's liquor in a gingerly fashion. The older man had never offered to share it. "And now you're dead," Oliphant informed the factor's ghost with some satisfaction. The Scotch rolled down his throat like a velvety fireball, trailing a sweet heat. He continued, "Sooner or later, the ice holding her chunk to another one is going to melt. Then her chunk will just slip into the lake. Then ... I don't know. Float around? Sink?"

He retired to the crude armchair that had been fashioned out of a biscuit barrel and stuffed with a sack of cedar shavings, with the sticky bottle of whisky in hand. The chipmunk babies, now nearly grown, frolicked on the counter and danced about the base of the brass beam scale.

The thought that the thaw would eventually dispose of the body for him was a great comfort. So much so that he poured himself another jigger of whisky. And then another.

"She's only an Indian," he reminded himself.

Oliphant awoke to loud cracks of thunder and the rat-a-tat of rain drumming against the tarpaper roof. His head felt squeezed in a vice, and when he rose from the cot, his feet looked much too far away to be his. Pulling on his coat over his long johns, he drew the bolt on the door and shuffled onto the porch. Overnight, large cracks had begun to appear in the ice that covered the lake. Now the wind drove these big chunks of ice first against the shore, then against one another, grinding them to fine, green dust. A quarter-mile to the north, a jack pine, which had been struck by lightning, burned bright orange against the black sky. All around the trading post, as far as Oliphant could see, rolled a flat of sliding, shining black mud. The factor's apprentice returned inside to light the coal-oil lamp and await the dawn.

As Oliphant suspected, the storm had greatly reduced the size of the dam. However, the block of ice that encased the girl was still intact. Carefully, he crawled out onto the dam and peered into it.

Strange, he marvelled. The girl didn't appear dead. After all, Oliphant had seen dead things, and all of them had looked dead. Stiff and white and empty somehow, like a discarded husk or an abandoned carapace.

The girl, on the other hand, looked as though she were sleeping. Was it possible that she was alive? Perhaps she had fallen into the icy river and frozen before actually drowning. Perhaps she could be revived, provided that her unthawing was handled properly. Certainly he had heard of people who were pronounced dead and later awakened, as hale and hearty as the next fellow. And wasn't someone buried alive every now and again? A terrible thought, to be buried alive.

All this thinking made Oliphant's sick headache worse; his heart fluttered and bumped unevenly in his chest, and he felt at once sick and faint. Moaning, he closed his eyes and edged backwards off the ice dam. Sinking down onto a boulder, he spread his knees wide and hung his head between them. Later, once his nausea had subsided, he sat up again and gazed out on the dark, curled shape of the girl caught in the block of green ice.

She had people somewhere who must be wondering where she is, he thought; perhaps they were unsure as to whether she had died or just run off. If he did nothing, let her slip away into the lake and downriver, they would never know for sure. How terrible it would be not to know! If only he could pry her free somehow and keep her until the Indians came back to the post, then he might find out who she was, who her people were, and let them know. The Indians always came back after the thaw, McGillvary had said. That's when they brought their furs to trade. Someone was bound to know who she was or if anyone had gone missing. But how to separate her chunk of ice from the others?

Oliphant returned to the post and, selecting two pieces of thick jack pine from the woodpile, went inside. He pulled the flannel sheet off McGillvary's bed and ripped it into strips, which he wrapped around the ends of the firewood, lashing them in place with codline. Then he went out back to the cold room and dipped each of the improvised torches into the barrel of coal oil. He set the saturated torches in an empty paint tin and tucked the following items in his packsack: a tin matchbox, a chisel, a hammer, a box of eight-inch spikes and a thirty-foot coil of the heaviest hemp rope he had in the store. Then he pulled on his hobnailed boots for extra traction, took up the packsack, went onto the porch, dragged his Wellingtons up and over the top of his other boots and, slipping his arms through the straps, adjusted the packsack to fit into the small of his back. Finally, he took his pick in one hand and the handle of the paint tin in the other and made his way back to the dam.

When he arrived on the shore, he slipped off the Wellingtons, tucked the pick up under the straps of the packsack, clamped the handle of the paint tin between his teeth and crawled out onto the slippery ledge. When he reached the chunk with the girl inside, he set down the paint can, removed the pick and placed it to one side, slipped off the packsack, unloaded it and started to work.

First, he chiselled out a line. Then he removed one of the torches from the paint can, lit it and drew the flame carefully along the chiselled line to melt a groove in the ice. He was very careful not to melt too much of the ice; it was his intention to keep her, after all, not to unthaw her. Then he took up his chisel again. Within the hour, between the torches and his chisel, Oliphant had separated from the dam a block of ice containing the girl.

He then drove three spikes into each side of the block and knotted the rope around them using granny hitches so they wouldn't slip. Finally, he knotted the rope around his own waist and, bracing himself and digging into the ice with the hobnails in his boots, eased the block off the ledge onto the lake's surface, which was still frozen around the dam but rotten in other places. It was a drop of a foot and a half. The ice sagged and creaked under the block's weight but, to Oliphant's relief, did not break.

The apprentice crawled backwards off the ice dam to the shore, taking care not to tangle or put too much strain on the rope tethered to the block. He planned to let the ice work for him, to not so much drag as slide the block to dry land. Accordingly, once on the bank, he pulled the Wellingtons back over top of his other boots, rechecked the knots and then began to walk slowly along the shore, easing the block of ice after him over the frozen, fragile surface of the lake. Because the ice was candled, however, making it needle sharp in places, Oliphant had sometimes to yank and bump the block along; in other places, the ice buckled and groaned under the block's weight, several times falling away just seconds after he had slid it clear, making a tinkling sound like glass shattering.

Finally, Oliphant arrived at the point on the lakeshore nearest the trading post. The ice had shrunk away from the shoreline here; he would have to float the block across. Bracing himself, he pulled the block off the ice and into the frigid, black water. It bobbed for a second, foundered, then began to sink. Summoning what remained of his limited strength, Oliphant heaved the block back up towards the surface, and wading out to it, he grasped a spike in each hand and shouldered it to shore. Then he half dragged, half shoved it the twenty feet to the ice house — this was a ramshackle, windowless hut resembling a woodpile that McGillvary, in his more sanguine years, had kept stocked with ice from the lake. Unfortunately, the factor's depression and subsequent obsession with rodents had so distracted him from his usual activities that, at present, there was only a little pile of ice in the middle of the shed, the remnants of the previous winter's haul.

Oliphant fashioned a kind of bier out of river rocks and levered the block onto it with a crowbar. He spent the rest of the day cutting and hauling ice, which he packed around the back and sides of the block. He left one side exposed, however — the one through which he could see most clearly the girl suspended in the cloud of her dying breath. Perhaps he would cover it too, he thought, but later.

"The ice will last until July," he remembered the factor telling him, "if there's enough of it."

Billy Big Blood came through in late May. He was looking for a prospector from the South Porcupine area who had gone missing in the bush. He had left his shack down on Pearl Lake six months ago, never to return; lately, his wife had grown anxious.

Oliphant showed him the girl. "Well?" he asked expectantly. "Is she one of yours?"

"Don't recognize her," Billy Big Blood said. "No one has gone missing —"

"Of course it's hard to tell," Oliphant jumped in, "the way her hair hangs in her face. Perhaps another tribe upriver . . ."

But Billy Big Blood was uneasy. "I don't know about this," he said, shaking his shaggy head. "She looks like a nebaunaube to me, the way her legs are folded."

"What do you mean?" asked Oliphant, hunkering down next to the block of ice and staring into it. "I mean, what was that you called her?" he clarified.

"A nebaunaube," replied Billy. "A sleep-being. That is a woman who lives in the lake and is part Anishinabe, part fish. Sometimes, in storms, a nebaunaube swims to the surface of the lake and pretends that she is drowning. 'Help! Help!' she cries. When a man comes to rescue her, she pulls him under the waves and marries him."

"Ah!" said Oliphant. "You mean a mermaid." The fishermen of Ayr had spoken of mermaids.

"A nebaunaube," Billy Big Blood articulated the word carefully. This white man! He couldn't pronounce anything properly.

"She doesn't have a fishtail," Oliphant pointed out, standing.

Billy shrugged. "A nebaunaube can look like a Anishinabe if it suits her," said Billy Big Blood. "Besides, the way her legs are, they could be webbed, like the feet of a duck."

"She looks as though she is sleeping," commented Oliphant dreamily. "Tell me, don't you think she looks alive?"

"The nebaunaube visit the Living World in dreams sometimes," Billy Big Blood conceded.

"Then they are like ghosts?" Oliphant asked. "Dead?"

"To live among the nebaunaube you must pass through four levels of life . . . or death, depending," explained Billy Big Blood.

"Depending on what?" Oliphant asked.

"On how you look at it," said Billy. "What are you going to do with her?"

"What would you do with her?" Oliphant asked.

"I would put her back in the lake," said Billy Big Blood. "I would not like to pass through four levels of life or death. At any rate, not just now. I am too busy trying to find this prospector."

"I think I will keep her," resolved Oliphant. "The rest of the Indians will be coming back soon. Perhaps one of them will recognize her."

Billy Big Blood shrugged. He did not know whether to tell the factor's apprentice that this year, for the first time in thirty years, his people were summering down on Nighthawk rather than at Frederick House Lake. Étienne, the French trader there, had cut them a good deal on their furs, and besides, there was better fishing at Nighthawk. Pickerel. "Have it your way," he told the white man. "But don't say I didn't warn you."

When it was dark, Oliphant lit the coal-oil lamp and set it next to the ice-house door so that the heat would not cause the block to sweat overmuch — he had taken to spending long hours with the ice woman while he waited for the Indians to return to the post. The block was smaller now, pitted and slippery. A scant two inches of ice separated the frozen girl from the soft June air. Now that so much of it had melted, he could see more clearly the pale patches of frostbite that covered the girl's skin, the cracks and lesions. He could see that toes were missing and fingers. Still, she seemed to him beautiful in the warm golden light of the coal lamp, all her parts round and folded as in sleep, his woman in ice.

Where were the Ojibwa? he wondered. When would they come?

A moment later, it occurred to Oliphant that the girl had moved. He straightened up, startled. Perhaps it was a trick of light, a reflection . . . or had the girl crooked a finger or drawn a knee a fraction of an inch closer to her chest? Oliphant, his heart squeezed tight as a fist, grappled for the lamp from beside the door and, hunkering down, swung it close to the block. A glint of brown through her streaming hair where there had never before been one.

Oliphant leapt to his feet, nearly dropping the lamp, and started back in terror.

The girl had opened her eye.

Billy Big Blood stopped by Frederick House Lake in July on his way back to Nighthawk. He had not found the prospector. He did not find Oliphant either or the woman in ice. Both were gone. Later, when the company wanted Billy to look for the apprentice, the big Indian demurred.

"I won't find him," he explained.

"But why not?" they demanded.

"He is with the nebaunaube," Billy said.

"What?" they asked.

TRAPLINES

Jean-Claude Villars ran his traplines north of Kamiscotia Lake, up as far as Upper Footprint Lake and Whitepine Hill and as far east as Moberly and Byers Lake. It took him upwards of a week to walk those lines, to tend the little houses of death that his wife, Mimi, had fashioned for him out of poles and spruce boughs, and to extract his prey from their fatal portals before rebaiting the traps with chunks of putrid whitefish and dribbles of catnip oil — lures to draw in the foxes and the martens and the minks whose furs he would stretch and cure and later sell to that new Frères Revillon outfit down in Timmins.

Of course, some years back, before gold had been

discovered at the Porcupine and silver at Cobalt and all those people had come rushing into these northern forests, trapping the whole country out or else driving the animals even deeper into the bush, Jean-Claude had sold his furs green — uncured and unstretched — to the Hudson's Bay factor . . . and made a better dollar on them, too. Only a man who had been at it as long as he had, forty years now since he was a boy, who had a system and worked it, could make a living trapping any more.

While Jean-Claude saw to the lines, Mimi Villars stayed back at their sturdy cabin on the northeastern shore of Kamiscotia Lake, ministering to their three-year-old daughter, Yvette. Before Yvette's birth, Mimi had accompanied her husband on his long journeys along the lines and fared none the worse for it. Her father had also been a trapper; life in the bush was what she knew.

However, little Yvette was not so hardy as her parents. From birth, she had been given to congestions and terrible rheums; she had a weak chest. "*Le bon Dieu* must have been short-winded when He blew the breath of life into you, *petite princesse*," Mimi worried aloud to Yvette as she smeared the little girl's shallow chest with bear grease to counteract vapours and draughts and the unseen spectres of contagion that laced the night air. Then she rolled a hot stove iron in thick layers of old flannel and dropped it into a woollen sock, which she placed at the foot of Yvette's cot. As a final precautionary measure, she made a small tobacco offering to Earth Mother, she who nourishes and clothes and shelters and heals. "Thank you, Muzzu-Kummik-Quae," Mimi whispered, "for not taking my little daughter away just yet."

Mimi's name was, in fact, Meemee — Ojibwa for "pigeon" — or at least that was what her mother's mother had told her. For Mimi was only a quarter-French. Her mother had been Anishinabe; her father half-French, half-Cree. He had trapped to the west of Halfmoon, up around Blue Lake and Winter Lake, and it had been at the Winter Lake camp that Mimi had met and, after a fashion (for there was no priest available), married Jean-Claude Villars fourteen years earlier. It had been late autumn, and Jean-Claude had been passing through from Flying Post with a dogsled full of moose meat and a side of caribou when her father had invited him to stop the night. A week later the trapper, who was then in his late thirties, left for Kamiscotia, taking eighteen-year-old Mimi with him. She hadn't seen her family often after that, and now they were all dead. There are many things to kill a person in the bush: typhoid and exposure, not to mention the death met by her favourite brother, Gilles, who was struck by lightning.

Yvette was Mimi and Jean-Claude's only child, born when they had been married more than a decade.

"*Quelle surprise!*" exclaimed Mimi. "A real *tah-hau*, as my grandmother would have said: *incroyable!*"

"Who would have thought such a thing possible?" agreed Jean-Claude. "After so many years, well . . . I thought for sure you were barren."

"And I am very old," marvelled Mimi.

Thinking it unlikely that they would be twice blessed in the matter of offspring, the Villars gave Yvette every attention. They were terrified that she would abandon them as suddenly and unpredictably as she had blessed them with her advent. If she caught a cold, they would lie awake half the night, her small, frail body pressed between their strong, wiry ones, willing her to breathe. If she ran a fever, Jean-Claude would hitch up the dogs and mush into Timmins for Dr. Jakes while Mimi furiously tended the child with lobelia emetics and bitterroot physics . . . until finally Dr. Jakes refused to come to Kamiscotia for anything less than pneumonia. It was as though Yvette's life force was some-how less substantial than that of other children — gossamer, easily rent. It was as though they could prevent the child from sliding away from them into silent death only by the constant exercise of extreme vigilance.

About once a week over the past year, Joe Hopcroft, a young neighbour, had stopped by the Villar place to smoke a pipe with Jean-Claude or, when the trapper was working his lines, to check up on Mimi and Yvette. Sapling-thin with a long, pale, foolish face, lank brown hair and watery blue eyes (red-rimmed much of the year from allergies), Joe was uncommonly lonely and forlorn, for he lived with Cyrus Moss, a terrible villain, and so had to seek out other company in order to enjoy agreeable conversation.

In addition to having been raised in a houseful of women, Joe had suffered severely from rheumatic fever as a child, with the result that he had a weak heart. Gentle, awk-ward and modest, he nevertheless half expected and cer-tainly hoped that solicitous and motherly females would pamper him and fuss over his health. Mimi, sinewy, brown and terse though she was, was the closest such female in these parts — Maggie Sinclair living on the other end of the lake and being as noisy as a duck in water, all the time clacking away — and Mimi always had a poultice of honeysuckle leaves for his blackfly bites or powdered myrtle bark for him to sniff to relieve his eternal catarrhs or tea made of purple foxglove for those frightening moments when his heart would flutter like a swallow trapped in a chimney pipe and not stop. As for Yvette, with her tiny hands and feet and her teeth like a scattering of seed pearls, she made him think of his littlest sister, Margaret, when she was that age.

"See here, Mademoiselle Villar!" he advised the child, setting her precariously on his skinny knee. "If you ain't very careful, I will surely marry you when you grow up!"

How Joe came to be on Kamiscotia was this: The winter before he had been passing through the area with some Hudson's Bay fellows bound for James Bay — several months earlier he had answered a newspaper advertisement and consequently signed up to apprentice as a factor in the company. He had felt that it was high time that he provided some solid financial support to his ageing mother. Besides, he was damned if his weakened heart, which had kept him from roughhousing with boys throughout his youth or doing anything strenuous at all, was going to stand in the way of his being a man. Well, that was Joe's idea.

He and his fellow-travellers stopped the night with Cyrus P. Moss, who lived directly across the lake from the Villars. In the process, Cy got poor Joe so drunk on homebrew that he managed to talk him into staying on with him as his trapping partner. "It's slave labour, working for the company!" he told Joe. "You'd make more money trapping in one season than you'd make in five years clerking for the company!"

Now why Cy Moss thought he wanted — or needed — a trapping partner was a mystery. He had long since ceased to run traplines himself. And why, given the fact that he himself no longer trapped for furs, he had chosen poor, weak, sickly Joe Hopcroft as his partner was a second mystery. But then, Cyrus Moss was a mysterious man.

He had come up to New Ontario a dozen years earlier, together with his brother Ivar and Ivar's wife. As for his place of origin, he told everybody a different story: that they'd come all the way up from southern Missouri; that they had owned a little farm in the Red River valley of Oklahoma; that he and his brother had raised corn and wheat on a hundred acres in Nebraska.

Given all this discrepancy, the folks around Kamiscotia thought it highly likely that the Mosses were running from the law; certainly they had that air about them — of being wary and suspicious, of covering their tracks.

"Still and all, I'd wager they were farmers once," commented Maggie Sinclair. "I seen 'em washed up, and even then they look dirty. Soil's too deep in their pores for soap to wash it out." It was true. The heavy-set, hard-bodied Moss men had that swarthiness peculiar to dirt farmers; it was as though they had been not so much burned by the sun as deeply and fundamentally stained by the land.

Ivar's wife was a mongrel — half-Negro, perhaps, or maybe part Indian. She was dark-skinned and had straight, long black hair that was always matted with straw and burrs and twigs from the forest. She spoke nothing resembling English. Indeed, nobody could untangle what exactly her name was from the jumble of syllables she let loose whenever people asked her, "How're you called?" As for Cy, he called her Katya, or sometimes Kattra, when he didn't call her the woman. Of course, Katya might have had some kind of speech impediment and been speaking English all along.

Cy and Ivar came to blows regularly. Once, Cy set Ivar on fire, and he saved himself only by jumping into the lake through a hole sawed in the ice for fishing. He nearly drowned in the icy water, and afterwards took a dose of pneumonia so bad it was doubtful he would live. Another time, Cy chopped off Ivar's thumb with an axe for spoiling an otherwise good caribou skin with an ill-placed shot.

Finally, Ivar just up and cleared out. Disappeared. This was going on four years ago. He either forgot his wife or else he remembered not to take her. Maggie Sinclair swore up and down that Katya was poisoning her husband slowly by mixing minute amounts of copper vitriol in his food. "That's why he always looks so greenish," she explained. "My guess is that she really wants to be with Cy," she continued. "Well, there's no accounting for taste." In any case, no one ever saw Moss's brother again.

After Ivar's departure, Cy and the woman lived together until her death a couple of years later. Nobody thought much about the arrangement one way or the other. Katya seemed to folks scarcely human — more like a dog than a woman, craven and always slinking about the edges of things. Likely Cy beat her, and that was what made her so fearful. Needless to say, when at last she died, there was some speculation that Cy might have done her in.

"I reckon he walloped her to death with a shovel," speculated Jean-Claude. "Or an axe."

"I think he shot her," Maggie opined.

"He probably didn't bury her at all," said Albert Fauteau. "Just tied stones to her feet and threw her into the lake."

For there had been no witnesses to either Katya's death or her burial, nor had there been word of any illness. Cy claimed that she had died suddenly in the night, and that he had buried her out back the following morning. "How do I know what killed her?" he demanded irately. "One minute she's alive and the next she's dead. Just died. Not a peep out of her."

After his sister-in-law's death, Cy Moss grew even harder to get along with than before. He squabbled with everyone he had dealings with, and conceived and then nurtured with the utmost diligence and exactitude elaborate grudges against first one neighbour, then another.

One night, out of spite or possibly out of revenge for some real or imagined slight, he plucked all of Maggie Sinclair's Rhode Island hens. When she stepped out into the dooryard the following morning to feed them, there the poor plucked creatures were — not red and black, as is proper to a Rhode Island hen, but naked as newly hatched chicks and stubbly. Half of them died of exposure before the day was out, for it was closing in on October at the time.

Another time, he knocked over the Fauteaus' outhouse. It seems he had a quarrel with their horse.

There was something else that happened after Katya's death: Cyrus Moss appeared to grow larger. He had never been a small man, but now he seemed taller than people remembered him being — by a good two or three inches.

"Probably he just seems bigger," speculated Murray Sinclair, Maggie's husband.

Jean-Claude disagreed. "Used to be I could look Cy Moss in the eye," he pointed out. "Now I have to look up at the bastard."

"Well, maybe you got smaller," Murray developed his hypothesis still further. "People do shrink, you know. When they get older."

Jean-Claude glared at him. He was fifty-two years old and somewhat sensitive about his age. "I was five foot eight when I was twenty-one and I'm five foot eight now," he insisted.

"I thought he grew some after that brother of his went away," remembered Maggie. "But I reckoned it was just that my recollection of him was poor. I'll tell you one thing: he don't eat proper now that that woman is gone. Thin as a rail and the colour of something a churchyard would cough up."

Six months after Katya's death, the lady bartender at the blind pig in Timmins refused to serve Moss any more on account of his language — less colourful than it was boorish — and the fact that he picked fights idly and to pass the time, like some men pick at a banjo or a guitar.

Accordingly, Cy began to brew his own beer up at Kamiscotia Lake. After that, he rarely left his cabin except to beat the bush for ptarmigan or to fish the lake for pickerel or to check his snares for bush rabbits. On these expeditions, he carried a loaded pistol, which he jammed into an inside pocket of his stiff, dirty overalls or into the pocket of his soiled Red River coat. This was in case he met an enemy. According to him, he had plenty of them.

"All Cy does day in, day out is make beer and drink it," Joe complained to Mimi. "I'd set up traplines and work them myself, but I don't know how and he sure enough isn't going to show me. Do you think Jean-Claude would take me with him next time?"

On another occasion, he told Mimi, "Sometimes I think that if I have to spend one more night with that foul-mouthed old drunk, I'll haul off and shoot him with his own pistol. Last night, he sat by the fire and swore at me so that I didn't sleep a wink. He swore at me for six solid hours, Madame Villars. One oath after another. Where does he learn them all? I think he makes some up, and I tell you, they're powerful oaths!"

Joe had dark circles under his eyes and his face was haggard and a yellowish pale beneath the snowburn, the colour of an old bruise; he looked exhausted.

"You need a tonic," Mimi observed. "I've got some of that Eclectic Oil I'll let you have. Well, then . . ." She poured condensed milk in his tea. It dripped reluctantly, chunkily, half-frozen. "Why do you stay with him?"

But Joe was thinking about the gun. "I know just where I'd put it," he said eagerly. "I've thought it all through. In his mouth when it's open and he's swearing at me. Then I'd squeeze the trigger and blow his brains all over the wall."

"And then they'd hang you," Mimi pointed out, stabbing the crystallized contents of the milk can with a knife to break them up.

One Thursday afternoon in late December, Joe decided to stop by the Villars homestead on his way back to Moss's cabin. He had snared a couple of bush rabbits and reckoned

Mimi might like one of the bitter-tasting creatures for her and Yvette's supper. It was going onto half past four, and the sun was riding the horizon in a pale, disorganized, pinkish blur when Joe wandered, whistling, towards the clearing in which the Villars' cabin was situated — this was about one hundred feet up from the lake's shore and on a bit of a rocky rise, to protect the house and its outbuildings from spring flooding, for the lake was creek-fed and rose a good ten feet in the thaw.

Just as he was coming around a loop in the trail and starting to climb the rise, he heard a terrible commotion coming from the direction of the cabin — shrieks, curses and high-pitched barking. Joe paused for a moment, his heart constricting with sudden fear. Mimi and Yvette! he thought. Were they being attacked? "Wait! Wait! Hold on!" he shouted, and dropping the two bush rabbits to the ground, he clamoured awkwardly up the slippery rise. "I'm coming! Hold on!" Joe attained the top of the rise and burst through the trees into the clearing. Then he stopped in his tracks. A sudden snow squall had rolled in off the lake, driven by a sharp, cold wind. Through the swirling snow and in the half-light, he could barely make out two heaving shapes in the dooryard. At first, he thought they might belong to two black bears on their hind legs, one big, one smaller, wrestling, but after blinking and shading his eyes and stumbling closer, he realized that the smaller shape belonged to Mimi Villar and the larger to his trapping partner, Cy Moss. Evidently, Cy had come up behind Mimi and seized her around the waist. Now he was attempting to drag her towards his toboggan, which was parked on the far side of the clearing. As for little Yvette, she was standing, frozen with terror, on the porch. At the sight of Joe, she raced down the steps and ran shrieking towards him, her arms outspread.

"What's this? What's going on?" Joe demanded, just before Yvette hurled herself at his knees, causing him to stagger backwards.

The sled dogs, already barking and yelping and leaping in their traces for excitement, wagged their tails at the sight of Joe and, throwing back their heads, howled with renewed enthusiasm.

"Cyrus Moss!" Joe yelled. "What in the blue blazes are you up to now?"

"Joe, help me!" cried Mimi, who was thrashing this way and that at the same time as she yanked at Moss's hands in an attempt to break his grip.

"'What in the blue blazes . . .'" Moss sneered in imitation of his partner. "God, but you're a milquetoast, Hopcroft! Stop wiggling, woman! Stop wiggling, I tell you! Like trying to wrestle a goddamned alligator! As for you, mama's boy . . ." He glanced briefly in Joe's direction. "Get the hell gone. You don't want to be messing with my business." His words swam loosely together and his stink reached Joe's nose across the clearing — Moss reeked of old, mouldy clothes that he had urinated in and of hops.

"Let her go, Cy," Joe advised his partner, trying gently to break Yvette's grip on his legs. "Come on, Vettie. Let go," he urged the little girl. To Moss, he said, "You're drunk."

"Don't tell me what to do, Hopcroft," Moss warned him.

"She ain't your wife, Cy!" Joe pointed out. Succeeding at last in breaking Yvette's grasp on his knees, he pushed her behind him and strode across the clearing. He took Moss by the arm and pulled at it. "Let her go, Cy!" he repeated.

"I ain't leaving till I get what I came for," Moss insisted.

Having to deal with Joe, however, split his focus, and Mimi, feeling his grip on her momentarily slacken, brought her hobnailed boot down hard on his left foot and tumbled free of his embrace. Picking up her skirts, she dashed around Moss and behind Joe. Snatching Yvette up into her arms, she retreated to a distance of some dozen feet.

Joe took a step backwards and extended his arms to either side, in a gesture both protective and conciliatory. "Now, Cy . . ." he began.

"I'll kill you, you half-breed bitch!" Moss raged, shaking his big fist at Mimi. Then he turned to Joe. "But first I'll kill you, Hopcroft, you goddamned, wet-behind-the-ears, grizzling, weaselling whelp!" He fumbled inside his coat for the pistol that he kept hidden there. "I'll shoot you is what I'll do," he continued, patting his pockets furiously. "Now where did I put the goddamned thing?"

At this, Mimi shrieked and pointed to the ground at Joe's feet. The pistol's butt poked lopsidedly out of the snow. It must have fallen out of Moss's coat during the struggle.

"What?" Moss wondered, frowning.

However, by the time he had managed to focus his gaze sufficiently to make out just what it was that Mimi was pointing to, Joe had scooped the pistol up and trained it on him. "I got the gun, Cy," he advised his partner, slowly releasing the safety. He felt a warmth invade his blood, as if quicksilver was being released into his veins. "Best go on home now," he said in a low, thrilling voice that he almost did not recognize.

"Got the gun! Got the gun!" Moss mocked, advancing on the younger man. "You lily-livered . . ."

Joe closed his eyes and squeezed the trigger. The gun exploded, flinging him backwards. The bullet ricocheted, burying itself in a jack pine. Joe could see that it had bitten off half of Moss's left ear in the process. "Well, golly!" he exclaimed.

"His ear!" cried Mimi.

"What . . . ? My ear?" Moss reached up to touch the side of his head and brought back a hand sticky with hot blood. "What'd you do to my ear?" he asked Joe. "Jesus, Joe, you blew my damned ear off!" He turned to Mimi. "He shot off my goddamned ear," he told her. "How does it look? You wouldn't happen to have a mirror, would you?"

As Mimi was washing up after supper, she heard a knock at the door. Because of the incident that afternoon, she had taken the unusual precaution of locking the door and drawing the bolt. Out here in the bush there was usually no need for such security measures. Besides, Jean-Claude's sled dogs could usually be counted on to raise the alarm. Of course, Jean-Claude had had need of the sled, and so had taken the dogs north with him. He had also taken the rifle, though he had left the shotgun.

Glancing through the window, she noticed that another snow squall had blown up from the lake, lightening the darkness to a hazy grey. The wind howled and shrieked around the little cabin; it clanked in the stove-pipe like something desperate to escape its creosote-lined confines.

Drying her red, chilblained hands on her apron, Mimi walked close to the door and, inclining forward, called through it, "Who is it?"

She fully expected to hear Joe Hopcroft's reedy voice pipe up in reply. He had loaded his partner into the toboggan and driven him home about an hour after sunset. This was after a dejected but fascinated Cy had made a thorough inspection of his ruined ear in her little hand mirror. Now the younger man was probably coming back for a visit after having put Cy to bed. Or maybe Cy had driven him out with his curses.

"Who is it?" she repeated.

"Well, it's Cyrus P. Moss," came the muffled reply.

Mimi started in surprise. Then, struggling to regain her composure, she leaned closer to the door and said, "Go away!"

"Who is it, Mama?" Yvette called anxiously. Mimi had just tucked her into her little cot. She had taken a long time to settle, what with the upset. "Who's at the door?"

"Shhh!" Mimi advised her. Then, in a louder voice, she repeated, "Go away, Cy! The door's bolted and the shotgun's loaded."

"Let me in, missus!" Cy pleaded. "I won't hurt you!"

"Mama!" Yvette sat up in her cot, pushing her blankets to one side. "Is it the terrible bad man?"

"It's young Joe, missus!" insisted Cy. "He's sick! He's . . . well, he's real sick!"

"Sick with what?" Mimi asked.

"How should I know?" Cy asked.

"I don't believe you!" Mimi told him. "You're just trying to get me to open the door. Yvette! Stop that grizzling!"

"Please, missus, I know I was . . . out of line this after-noon," Cy said. "I go crazy when I get to drinking. I'm sober now, though. The sight of poor Joe sobered me up real quick, I tell you. He's calling for you, missus. You have to come. Please! I was out of my head earlier. It'll never happen again. But now . . . will you help me, missus?" His rusty, jagged voice cracked. "Will you come and help poor Joe?"

Mimi hesitated. Moss did sound sober, and he sounded contrite as well. There were people, she knew, who went crazy when they drank but were all right otherwise. "Joe's really sick?" she asked sternly.

"Oh, yes," Cy assured her. "I'd say he's as sick as they get!"

"I can't leave Yvette," Mimi said.

"We can take the littl'un with us," offered Cy.

"It's not a fit night for travelling."

"Don't you worry, missus. I got my feather robe right here in the sled. The both of you can roll up in that, and I'll drive the toboggan. You'll be warm as toast. But we have to hurry."

"Oh . . . oh . . . oh, all right," Mimi conceded at last. "But you wait out there while I get Yvette ready."

Despite her misgivings, she got the little girl out of bed and, over her howled protests, began to dress her.

Outside the tiny, woodsmoke-smelling cabin, the northern lights leapt, blocking out stars as big around and bright as shining silver dollars, while the ice that capped Kamiscotia Lake growled and creaked like some great monster awakening and unfolding from its lair.

❧

By land, following the lake's shore, the Villars' homestead was separated from Moss's cabin by a good four miles. However, with the lake already frozen to a depth of four feet and covered with wind-packed drifts, it took only a half an hour to mush from the Villars' cabin to Moss's, in spite of the swirling, gusting snow and the persistent sharp wind.

Even under cover of darkness, Moss's cabin looked mean and hunkered down in its tiny triangle of half-cleared land — more like a hastily constructed duckblind than a human habitation. Cy and his brother had thrown it together in a couple of days — with that first cold winter up north blowing hard at their backs and no woodsman's skills to speak of — and little had been done to improve it since.

Cy reigned in the dogs before the cabin. Through near-blinding snow, Mimi could just make out that the door was half ajar: lantern light spilled through the crack onto the ground before the threshold, staining the snow a brassy yellow.

"He's sick, and you leave the door open? You want him to freeze?" Mimi demanded angrily. Leaping to her feet, she pulled Yvette after her.

Cy shrugged and bent down to unfasten the dogs' harness traces. He unfastened only one trace apiece, so that the dogs could lie down and rest but might be quickly reharnessed should he require them.

"Idiot!" Mimi fumed. She pushed the door open and strode into the cabin, dragging Yvette after her. She had not been at the Moss place for several years, certainly not since Cy's sister-in-law had died. It was a dark, frigid shambles. Gingerly, Mimi stepped over tumbled furniture to where the lit coal-oil lantern sat on the packed dirt floor beside a smoke-blackened wood stove. She picked it up and shone its light into the dark corners. The room smelled fetidly of brewing beer and something else. It was a potent, stale smell, slightly sweet. She sniffed hard, trying to place the odour. "Joe?" she called.

Moss lumbered into the cabin, his battered melton cap in his huge hands. Didn't he seem larger than he had that afternoon? Mimi wondered. By a good two or three inches . . .

"Mama!" Yvette cried suddenly, pointing to a crumpled, human-sized bundle, half-wedged between the far side of the stove and the wall.

Mimi inhaled sharply. Then she knelt down beside the stove and edged as far around it as she could fit. Trembling, she lifted the lantern high to get a better look at what Moss had jammed into the dark, cobwebby corner. By the lantern's yellow glow, she could just make out the features of Joe Hopcroft's face, frozen in an expression of intense surprise. She scuttled backwards and struggled to her feet. "What happened?" she demanded.

"He just grabbed his chest and fell over," Cy explained. "Before he did, he made the beatingest sound. Sort of a gurgle."

"You said he was sick!" Mimi cried.

"Well, yes'm, I did," conceded Cy.

"But he's dead!"

"I said he was real sick," Cy countered.

"Well, what were you doing when he grabbed his chest and fell over?"

"I had my pistol stuck in his ear," Cy replied.

"You frightened him to death! Didn't you know he had a weak heart?"

"Yes'm, I did," said Cy. "I reckoned if his heart didn't give out, I could just go ahead and shoot him."

Mimi stared at Cy's face in the lamplight. It was gaunt, the skin pulled tight over his cheekbones, and ashen, a corpse's dull, drained colour. He extended one bony, gnarled hand towards her. "Come here," he said gruffly. "No fussing now."

It was then that she recognized the odour she had been unable to place a few moments before — it was the smell of slow decay in a cold place. She retreated backwards, then, half-turning, heaved the coal-oil lantern at his chest. The glass chimney shattered on impact, kerosene splashed on Moss's jacket, and the tongue of yellow flame the lantern nursed leapt onto the fabric and wriggled excitedly along the line of the stain. Moss bellowed and, stepping back, began to pound his coat with his gloved hands in an attempt to put out the fire.

Mimi wheeled around on her heels, snatched Yvette up into her arms, ran to the door, flung it open and toppled outside. Stumbling across the clearing with the child, she reviewed her options: Moss would be after her any minute. There was no time to hitch up the dogs. If she attempted to escape the way they had come, across the lake, it would not take her long to reach home. However, the snow had ceased to blow and the moon had just risen, making the snow on the ice glow blue-white. There was no cover, nowhere to hide. Besides, how fast could she go, carrying the child? She glanced over to where the dogs lay curled up in the snow, noses tucked under tails. They gazed back at her with green, shining eyes. One dog sat up and tentatively barked. They were still bound together by their harness traces. It wouldn't take Moss long to hitch them up again. He would bring her down in no time on the lake.

But if she took the bush trail instead, the journey would take her at least an hour, probably more, and Yvette would surely take sick from exposure. Besides, she was sure to find the murderer at her cabin when she arrived, waiting for her, and there was no nearer neighbour to whom she could go. The Sinclairs lived at the far end of the lake, while the Fauteau place was deeper into the bush, near the rapids.

Mimi ran over to the toboggan, grabbed Moss's feather robe, flung it around Yvette, swung the little girl up into her arms and over her left shoulder, and started down the bush trail. He'll see my tracks and follow me, she thought. Once I am deeper into the forest, where the dense tree cover blocks moonlight and makes it harder to see, I'll duck off the path and cut through bush until I reach the shore. Then I'll head off across the lake for home. That way, there's a chance I'll get there before he does.

As she started down the path, Moss burst out of the cabin, pounding at his burning jacket with mittened hands. He fell to his knees, then pitched forward, rolling in the snow to extinguish the fire. "Shit!" he cried. "Shit! Damned woman tried to burn me up! Now where'd she go?"

Hurriedly, Mimi ducked under a low-hanging bough and then stumbled over a root half-buried in snow. He will be looking for my tracks now — she imagined his movements — now he's found them. Now he's trying to figure out whether to take the toboggan. Now he's deciding that he should — he has to carry me back, after all. Now he's running over to the dogs. Now he's rehitching their harnesses. . . . She figured that she had five, maybe ten minutes before he would start to close in on her.

"*Mama,*" Yvette whimpered. "*Il fait trop froid.*"

"Shush, angel! You must be so very quiet!" Mimi warned her in a whisper. "As quiet as your grandmama after she died."

She had come into a stretch of jack pine so dense that she could barely make out where the pitted, rooty path ended and the bush began. I should leave the path here, she told herself. Start for the shore.

Stepping from the path, Mimi began to force her way through the bush towards the lakeshore. It was hard going, particularly since she could not use her hands to clear the way. The underbrush was thick with deadfalls and windrows that snow and ice had rendered solid. She made her way cautiously around these lopsided domes — brown bears favoured such places for their winter dens, and she did not want to rouse a mother bear. Moreover, the feather robe in which she had wrapped Yvette kept catching on thorns and branches, and then she would have to stop and untangle it with just the one hand, pricking herself savagely in the process.

Finally, however, she did reach the little fringe of spruce and willow that lined the lakeshore. Before her the lake extended, shining blue-white in the bright cold moonlight like a freshly laundered sheet on a clothesline, its wind-packed drifts frozen in mid-undulation. Mimi stepped out onto the ice and, moving as quickly as she could without snowshoes, bore the shivering, whimpering child, whose weight increased with every step she took, across the lake towards the dark, distant home.

The journey took longer than she had hoped; Mimi was certain that Moss had beaten her home. Therefore, she did not go directly to the front of the cabin, which faced out onto the lake, but instead veered to the west and cut off into the bush again, coming up on the house by the back way. If Moss had parked himself in front of the cabin, she and Yvette could hide in the cowshed — the cow's body heat would serve to keep them warm for the night. Moss couldn't get in without the key, Mimi reasoned, not without breaking down the door, and Jean-Claude had built it sturdy, to withstand bears and other wild creatures. Surely Moss would leave when she didn't arrive. He would either go home or look for her elsewhere. That was what she figured.

Mimi deposited Yvette in the cowshed with strict instructions to be quiet no matter what, then she crept cautiously around the back of the house and peered into the clearing. Sure enough, the dogs were lying half-harnessed by the porch, and there in the toboggan, covered with a soiled rabbitskin robe and snoring raucously, was Moss.

Mimi tiptoed back to the cowshed, bundled Yvette back up in the feather robe and once again picked up the child, holding her to her chest so that the little girl's face rested against her left shoulder. Leaving the cowshed behind, she crept stealthily along the side of the house and around the front. It was all that she could do to breathe. Her heart had grown so huge inside her chest that it seemed to want to push its way out her throat; it left no room for air.

If only she could make it inside the cabin, she thought. If only he would not wake up. . . . Even through the feather robe, Yvette felt hot to her touch. Too hot. Did the child have another fever?

The lead dog started up, growling.

Mimi froze.

The dog cocked its head to one side, peering at her. Then it wagged its tail in recognition. The woman had petted it once; the dog wondered if perhaps she might give it food.

Suddenly, Moss stirred.

Mimi lay back against the side of the house, not moving.

Moss muttered something and made a few disjointed, smacking noises before rolling over in the rabbitskin robe to face away from the cabin and towards the lake. He was quiet for a moment, then he started to snore again.

Dizzy now with anxiety, Mimi slid past the interested dog and its master and up onto the cabin porch. She set Yvette on her feet, and with fumbling fingers, she extracted the key from her pocket and slid it into the lock. It turned with a loud, plosive creak. She threw open the door, pushed Yvette inside, fell in after her, then locked and bolted the door behind her. Then she barricaded both the door and the window with tables and benches and that big chiffarobe that had come down to Jean-Claude from his grandmother. She placed three axes, a pick, a gimlet, a butcher knife and a cleaver on the floor in the centre of the room so she could reach them in a hurry, and she set the loaded shotgun beside the bed, where it would be handy.

Then she took Yvette into her and her husband's bed and lay down beside her. The child was as hot as a stove, but after three hours in the freezing cold, Mimi could not bring herself to make compresses for the little girl, nor could she have gone outside to fetch the snow and ice she would have needed for them. She was trapped.

Moss awoke at daybreak and shuffled off into the bush to urinate. Then he helped himself to some of the firewood and kindling piled on the Villars' porch and built a big fire in the centre of the dooryard. Taking two battered pails and a tin teakettle from the front of the toboggan, he filled one with cornmush and cracklings for the dogs and set it to heat over the fire. The second he packed with snow. When the cornmush and cracklings started to bubble, he took them off the fire and set the pail of snow in their stead. Picking up the pail of mush and walking among the dogs, he poured a mess of it out onto the snow in front of each of them. When the snow in the second teakettle had melted and boiled, Moss made himself tea, sweetening it with condensed milk that he poured from a can stored in the grub box of his toboggan. Then he roamed around the dooryard, gripping his tin mug between his mittened hands and taking cautious sips of the steaming sweet tea while surveying the white face of the lake. Only then did he notice the tracks leading around the house to the porch steps. "Damnation!" he swore.

Inside, Mimi sat up in bed.

Moss loped up the porch steps and pounded on the door with his fist. "I know you're in there!" he shouted. "I seen your tracks." He decided to change tactics. "Please, missus," he said in a wheedling tone. "Let me in. I can explain everything." He waited a moment, then walked over to the window and tried to peer in. All he could make out was the wooden back of the chiffarobe, which she had pushed in front of the window the night before. He returned to the door. "I ain't going to hurt you none, missus! What happened to Joe was what you call self-defence! I wouldn't have pointed that gun at him if he hadn't pointed it at me first." He waited. "Well, I know you're in there!" he concluded and, dropping down the two steps off the porch, shuffled back across the dooryard to the fire. He poured himself another mug of tea and hunkered down in front of the fire to drink it.

Mimi lay back on the bed again, holding Yvette tightly to her. The little girl was burning with fever. She must think, think what to do for a fever when she had so little water. She had some balmony bitters in gin. That might help. And crawley-root tea . . . she could make a small amount of that.

Moss returned to the door. "What are you scared of, missus? Scared I'll shoot you and the little girl? I wouldn't do that. No. What's the point of doing that?" He pounded at the door with his fist. "Hello? Hello? Let me in!"

He dropped off the porch again and shambled back and forth across the dooryard, clapping and chafing his hands to keep them warm. The sun was clear of the horizon now, and its tender light spilled onto the lake, golden and pink. "Damn!" he swore to himself.

Once again, he clambered up onto the porch and battered at the door. Then he kicked it. "I'm not going to shoot you!" he advised Mimi. "Do you hear me, half-breed bitch? No! I don't shoot females. Do you want to know what I do to females? Do you want to know? It ain't going to hurt you none to oblige me. Do you hear me, missus? I'll tell you what. Your old man's on his traplines and he ain't coming back for days, and Joe Hopcroft's deader than Mr. Jesus himself. Ain't nobody going to help you." Grabbing a big piece of firewood, he slammed it against the door for emphasis.

"I've got enough food here to last me a month," Mimi lied.

"Yeah?" Moss retorted. "And how much water you got?"

In the toboggan, tucked away next to his grub box, was a frozen moose muzzle and, stored in dirty straw, a large wooden crate half filled with beer bottles. While Mimi took stock of what water and food she had and brewed some crawley-root tea for Yvette, using only as much water as she thought the little girl could get down, Moss set the crate down near to the fire to warm the bottles up and spitted the moose muzzle over the flames. "In case you're wondering," he called to Mimi, "I'm not going anywhere."

Once the beer bottles had defrosted somewhat, he began to drink again, bottle after bottle in quick succession. Every twenty minutes or so, he would lurch to his feet and stagger over to the edge of the forest to urinate into the bush. With every beer he consumed, this became increasingly problematical — the last time, he nearly lost his balance and keeled over into the scrub.

An hour passed, and the moose muzzle was ready to eat. Mimi could smell the rich, greasy meat through the thick cabin walls. Having eaten only a little oatmeal with condensed milk and some dried apples that morning, she was very hungry; as for Yvette, she had taken nothing but tea and a biscuit before falling back into a light, feverish sleep.

Lifting the spit off the fire, Moss ate the muzzle off the stick. Grease splattered his half-burnt coat and juice dribbled down his chin. "Surely does tastes good!" he advised Mimi. "Bet you two are plenty hungry for a good piece of meat like this here. Let you have some if you'll come out!"

After he finished his meal, Moss climbed into the toboggan and wiped his face and hands on the rabbitskin robe before settling it around him. Lying back in the toboggan, he fell asleep. An hour later, he awoke and started back in on the remaining beer. He was growing agitated now and surly. Instead of settling down next to the fire, he walked around and around the cabin, kicking the walls and shouting.

"How long do you think you can stay in there? Hey, missus?"

"You can't have much water left! Better come out now and get it over with!"

"Goddamn, woman, you'd better not make me mad or you'll live to regret it!"

Yvette slept and woke up and fell asleep and woke up shrieking. She was light-headed with fever, and Mimi could barely make out what she was saying.

Shortly after noon, Moss drank his last bottle of beer. "Shit!" he said to the dogs, peering blearily at the empty bottle in his hand. "What am I going to do now?" He sat and thought about it for a few minutes. Then he stood, swaying. "I'm leaving now!" he called to Mimi, "but I'm just goin' 'cross the lake. Ain't going to be but an hour. Don't you think of going nowhere, 'cause there's no place you can go in an hour that I can't find you with the dogs, so just . . . stay put till I get back!"

At that, he reharnessed the dogs, with some difficulty, and headed out across the lake for his own cabin.

Mimi waited a few minutes, then pushed the chiffarobe a few inches to one side so that she could see out the window. There was Moss's dogsled, disappearing across the white eye of the lake. He was right, of course. There was no place she could go in an hour. But how long could she hold out? More important, how long could Yvette hold out?

Hurriedly Mimi took up her axe and two buckets and scurried out to dig up snow to carry back to the house. She transferred a week's supply of firewood from the porch into the cabin and laid in a store of food from the cold house. Then she half dragged, half pushed the reluctant cow up the steps and through the door so that they could have milk. She was just crossing the dooryard with an armful of hay when she spotted the dogsled returning across the lake in a cloud of swirling snow.

That was when she remembered.

Her n'oko, her mother's mother, sat by the fire at the Winter Lake camp, keeping old bones warm while she stirred the sagamite. "*Kegoh zaum! Baenuk!*" the old woman warned the child Meemee. "Think of others! Balance, moderation, self-control! Otherwise a weendigo will surely get you!"

"A weendigo?" Meemee asked. "What is a weendigo?"

"A weendigo is a terrible manitou that lives deep in the forest and feeds upon the bones and blood and flesh of human beings," her n'oko advised her. "It eats them live, as some animals do, because they taste fresher that way."

Meemee shivered. "What does this weendigo look like?" she wanted to know.

"Oh, it is a bad-looking monster," her grandmother told her. "In fact, its appearance is so ghastly that one look at a weendigo will cause many victims to die of fright! For it looks like a corpse before the skin leaves it — all dry and ashen, with the bones pushing through, and as thin as a wolf during the cold moon! That's the thing about a weendigo, Granddaughter — it is always hungry. Hungrier than you have ever been in your life. Hungrier than you can imagine. And no matter how much it eats — even if it eats an entire village — it makes no difference: it is still hungry."

"How is that, N'oko?" Meemee asked. "How is it that the weendigo can never be full?"

"Well," her grandmother told her, "it's simple, really. Each time the weendigo eats a person, it grows taller. Weendigos can be seven or eight or even ten times the height of a normal man. And what would have satisfied a weendigo when it was seven feet tall will not suffice when it is ten feet tall. And so on."

"Where do weendigos come from?" Meemee asked. "Were they here when the world began?"

"No, I don't think so," N'oko told her. "For the things that were here when the world began do not change, and weendigos are forever changing. No, I think weendigos were once human beings, bad human beings who placed their own good and pleasure before that of the village. For that is how it starts out, Granddaughter. Later, you know that the bad person has become a weendigo because of the smell of decay that hangs around him, and wherever he goes, he travels in a cloud of snow."

When Moss drove the toboggan into the dooryard, Mimi, who had pushed the chiffarobe a little to one side so that she could peer through the window at him, could see that it was heavily loaded. The dogs strained under its weight and the tarpaulin bulged over its contents. Clearly, Moss was settling in for a siege.

Unlashing the tarpaulin, he extracted a frozen moose haunch from it. Then he hauled four big wooden crates out of the toboggan and proceeded to unload them — they were full of beer bottles packed in straw. He placed the bottles in a circle around the fire so they wouldn't freeze, opened one and sauntered up onto the porch.

"I'm back!" he yelled and kicked the door. "Hello there, missus! Ready to come out and play?" He kicked the door again. "No?" Grumbling and wiping his nose with his mittened hands, he selected four pieces of jack pine and some kindling from the pile of firewood beside the door — the fire he had built that morning had died back to embers during his absence. "Goddamn woman," he muttered.

He tended to the fire and drank a couple more beers. Then he staggered up to the porch. "Now, I know what you're thinking," he informed Mimi through the door. "You're thinking that I'll get tired of waiting and go away, but it won't happen. I'm like one of those bull mooses, you know, in the fall when they got just one thing on their mind and these big antlers. Well, I'm like one of those bull mooses. Yeah, and I got a mighty big antler. You want to see my antler? You want to see it, missus?" He felt around in his pants. "There it is," he said after a minute. "Thought it'd gone missing on me. It's kind of cold for the big antler, but you come over to the window and I'll make it big for you. No? Damn, woman, but you're hard to get along with."

And he returned to the fire.

Hours passed. With the coming of evening, Yvette's fever began to rise again. She slept fitfully, murmuring and tossing in Mimi and Jean-Claude's bed. To Mimi's horror, the child had begun to cough — a dry rattle like seeds in a pod. Please do not let it be pneumonia again! Mimi prayed, pressing a cloth dipped in ice water to her daughter's hot, dry forehead.

With the chiffarobe blocking the window and the sun sinking, it was dark inside the cabin and close. The cow bawled forlornly for hay; she had long since eaten what Mimi had fetched in from the shed. In addition, it was difficult to walk without stepping on a cow-pat.

Every half-hour or so, Moss would lurch to his feet and stagger around the cabin, banging on its walls with a bottle or kicking them, howling "The Jam on Jerry's Rock" and every other barroom song of which he knew the first verse. Sometimes he would come up on the porch and explain in great detail what he would do to her and how when he got her, following which he would kick the door until the entire cabin shook.

Then, when the sun had set and the cold had deepened and the stars shone big and bright, he started to include what he would do to Yvette in the litany. That was when Mimi decided to kill him.

According to her grandmother, it was possible to kill a weendigo. "Indeed," as N'oko had pointed out, "if it were not, there would be no people on the earth, for the weendigos would have long since eaten them all."

So Mimi placed her sharpest axe and Jean-Claude's pitchfork and the big cleaver and the twelve-gauge shotgun next to the door, and then she drew the three-legged cricket from its place beside the stove up next to the chiffarobe blocking the window. Peering through the crack she had made by shifting the chiffarobe a little to one side, she watched for an opportunity. Although night had fallen, the fire Moss had built illuminated the dooryard to the extent that she could make out shadows and shapes by its orange light.

Finally, just after seven o'clock at night, Moss, who had been drinking steadily now since just after sunrise, staggered over to the toboggan and collapsed heavily into it. After a few, disorganized minutes, during which he yanked and kicked the rabbitskin robe into place around him and cursed haphazardly, he fell silent. Moments later, he began to snore.

Mimi crept over to the bed and checked Yvette. The child slept in that suspended way the feverish do, on her back, her arms out to either side of her, her eyelids twitching. She looked as though she might, at any moment, levitate. Her breathing made a grating sound, as if her breath were being dragged over a rusty washboard. Mimi placed a cold hand on her hot, dry forehead, then traced the sign of the cross on the tender skin with her thumb.

Moving to the door, she dribbled a little machine oil from the can onto the bolt and then drew it, slowly, so that it would not make too loud of a squeak. She stepped out onto the porch. By the firelight, she could just make out the rounded shape of the sleeping dogs, the heap of Moss in the toboggan. Careful to avoid the creaking plank of poplar just before the door, she transferred her arsenal of weapons from the inside of the cabin to the porch. She leaned the pitchfork against the rail, placed the axe and the cleaver on the floor beside her, and set the box of shells at her feet. If she missed shooting him with the shotgun, she would attack him with the pitchfork, then the axe, then the cleaver. That was her plan.

Bracing her thigh against the post that held up the porch, she lifted the shotgun to her shoulder and peered down the sight at that part of the black shape that she hoped was Moss's head. She had never had to fire the shotgun before, although Jean-Claude had long ago showed her how. He kept the gun for bears or wolves, for creatures one intends to kill rather than skin or eat, since lead will spoil a good pelt or meat. The twelve-gauge was double-barrelled.

If she was quick about it, she could squeeze off both triggers before the recoil threw her off her balance.

Mimi steadied herself, planted her feet, took a deep breath and squeezed off both triggers of the shotgun.

There was a loud blast and smoke. The recoil spun her backwards and tossed her onto her rear end. The dogs started up, barking. Mimi scrambled to her feet, cracked the barrel and shoved in two more shells. Then she glanced up, towards the fire. There was no movement from the toboggan.

Once again she lifted the shotgun to her shoulder, braced herself, lined up in her sights what she thought had to be Moss's head and fired. This time, she was better prepared for the force of the recoil and caught herself against the rail before she fell.

When the smoke cleared, she could still discern no movement. She peered at the toboggan, but in the dim firelight it was impossible to make out anything beyond the still, black shape of him. She would have to go closer to find out whether she had managed to kill him.

Picking up the pitchfork, Mimi stepped off the porch and waded through the snow towards the toboggan, holding the pitchfork up and like a spear, with two hands. Her heart was beating so violently that she could feel it pulse in the muscles of her cheeks, and the sound her blood made rushing in her ears was so loud that she could barely hear the yelping of the sled dogs which, in their excited attempts to escape their traces, had tangled themselves up so thoroughly that they were falling all over each other. She circled around the front of the toboggan, holding the pitchfork back and ready as she leaned forward to peer at a mess of bone and blood and pulp on some kind of stalk. Reaching out with one hand, she jerked the blood-soaked rabbitskin robe clear of his body. There were his hands, folded on his stomach . . . his shoulders, his neck. She must have blown off his face and a good portion of his head. He must have died in his sleep, instantly, unaware of danger, unafraid.

"You should have been afraid!" Mimi told the eyeless mess. "You scared poor Joe to death and you scared me half to death! You should have been afraid! You should have suffered! You should have suffered the way I suffered!"

Lunging forward, she drove the tines of the pitchfork deep into Moss's bulky torso, jumping on the handle to push them in farther. Then, wading back to the porch, she seized the axe and the cleaver and returned to the toboggan. Shrieking, she flailed around the toboggan, the axe in one hand, the cleaver in the other, haphazardly hacking and slicing at Moss.

"Mama!"

Mimi stopped and turned slowly to look in the direction from which the voice had come, towards the porch.

Yvette was standing in the door. From across the yard, Mimi could see that she trembled. "Mama!" the child cried in a thin voice. "Blood!"

Mimi glanced down at her clothing — it was soaked with gore and bits of tissue. Her hair was matted with it. She looked around her. The snow for a three-foot radius around the toboggan was soaked with blood. Pieces of Moss's flesh and scraps of bloody fabric littered the ground.

Mimi fought for control, then said in a low voice, "It's all right, *princesse*. Mama was just killing the weendigo."

Yvette recovered from the pneumonia she contracted that cold December night in the bush with her mother, but she died two years later of whooping cough.

Mimi, who had taken Yvette to the Sinclairs' as soon as she was able to reharness the dogs and tumble the pulpy remains of Moss from the toboggan, remained there until Jean-Claude's return from his traplines several days later. By that time, wolves had eaten most of the weendigo.

In the spring, curious neighbours dug all around the Moss place, trying in vain to locate the body of Katya, Moss's sister-in-law. Nor was there ever any word of Moss's brother, Ivar. A few years later, however, an RCMP officer came through Timmins and Cobalt looking for a man wanted for a murder in Manitoba fifteen years back. He fit Cyrus Moss's description precisely, except for one detail: the Manitoba murderer had stood five feet, eight inches tall, whereas Moss's skeleton, when it was exhumed, measured a full six feet, seven inches.

THE UNCHARTED HEART

O f course he knew its coordinates, its longitude and latitude, where it lay in relation to other geographical features: east of Frederick House River and west of Prosser Lake, north of Gowanmarsh and south of Little Lake. It was not three miles from the Buskegau, although that river didn't feed it. Nor had it any other tributaries. It lay where the retreating ice had torn a hole in the shield and the rain had filled it, the little, oblong blue lake stranded in bush that had been called by no name for so long, only the Lake. . . . Yes, he knew exactly where the Lake was, had known it all along, even though he had not included it on the original survey of 1910, or on later ones, or for that matter, on his famous map or its first revision. He had known of its existence, its whereabouts, for more than a decade but told no one.

Years later, the old geologist lay in the oncology ward of the Toronto General Hospital, stretched out on his canti-levered bed like a man on a rack, each of his bones aching like a separate, sore tooth. Cancer had driven the marrow from them, spread in its place. His bones glowed like embers. McQuat had just started him on morphine, drip-ping through the IV tube into the popped blue vein of his skeletal left hand. McQuat was his doctor. The drug dis-tanced him from the pain, threw up a shimmering, trans-parent veil through which he observed himself dying in a darkened room; he noted the pain, even acknowledged that it was his, without actually participating in it. He felt light, blown, like a burst milkweed pod that teeters on its stalk towards the end of autumn, tugged by breezes. Soon the stalk would break and the geologist would tumble, end over end, across the meadow towards the river.

In the midst of all this floating, he suddenly remem-bered that he had a secret. How surprising! Not that he had ever really forgotten. The morphine had distracted him, had borne him up in soft arms and, beating its big angel wings, spirited him to a lofty vantage point from which he might look down on his past from a different angle. And there it is, he marvelled. A blue lake under a sky filled with clouds. A beautiful woman. An incurable sweetness like an illness that soothingly debilitates. A point not charted on a map until it was all over.

The knowledge of this thing he had done long ago had burned in him for six decades like a slow ground fire that gives off no smoke but consumes what lies beneath it.

Slowly. Inexorably. And now it had come to this: his death. The key question in his mind now was, Had it really happened or had he made it up?

His tongue stirred in his mouth, as sluggish and thick-blooded as a wintering snake. "Marguerite!" he managed.

Margie Macoun Dawkins glanced up sharply from the old issue of *Chatelaine* that she was struggling to read by the light that seeped through the door from the corridor — one-pot suppers and makeovers for tired bathrooms.

"What is it, Dad?" she asked.

She was a soft, spongy, middle-aged woman with pale, freckled skin. The freckles were the same colour as her hair — taffy — and her eyes behind the pink glasses flecked with gold were that bright blue that is sometimes described as china blue.

"So, you're here, then!" he exclaimed in a hoarse whisper. "My little Marguerite! And here I was wondering if I had made you up."

"I've been here since nine this morning, Dad," she replied wearily and a little sharply, too. "I'm here every morning by nine."

Her father's prolonged illness had poked her life full of holes, not that she had had much of a life since the divorce. Through these holes, what small store of love and patience she still possessed had slowly seeped away. Who would have thought it would take him so long to die? Of course, she corrected herself, it's that I hate watching him suffer. I would have preferred for him to die with dignity than this way, a hollow husk pumped full of drugs. Rising, she crossed to the bed, bent forward and touched the loose bag of bones that was his hand, grazed his bumpy forehead with her lips. "So . . . how are you feeling?" she asked more tenderly.

"Like a bird!" the geologist trilled.

Convinced that they could subordinate large-scale physical geography to human needs by applying the principles of geometry to it — and driven by a terrible urge to do so — the Victorians had already produced a rough map of New Ontario during the latter part of Queen Victoria's reign. However, since silver had been discovered in Cobalt in 1903 and gold in the Porcupine six years later, the government had commissioned more precise maps of the region, to facilitate claim-staking and the consequent collection of fees. Therefore, in 1910, the Bureau of Mines, which formed part of the Department of Crown Lands, dispatched a number of geologists north to collectively survey the region.

One of those geologists was George Dewey Macoun. He was twenty-six years old at the time, a graduate of Queen's University in Kingston. He had apprenticed for two years with the renowned Toronto firm of Deville, King and Klotz before signing on with the Bureau of Mines. George was tall and lanky, heavy-boned, a little stooped and possessed of a long, gaunt face that ran to exaggerated hollows, pits and protuberances. Sun- and windburn had already begun to toughen his skin, which, because of years of fieldwork, was tanned year-round. His eyes stared clear and hazel out of their pronounced sockets. Once, he had endeavoured to grow a set of gingery mutton chop whiskers (his hair, already thinning at the crown, was the dull dun colour of a mouse). When his master, Surveyor General Edoard Deville, remarked of these whiskers in passing, "It appears, Mr. Macoun, that you may have developed mange," George promptly shaved them off. It was to be his only attempt at self-adornment, although he was quite partial to the surveyors' quasi-military uniform of khaki, kerchief and Stetson hat.

George was engaged to marry Miss Frieda Eckert, a somewhat sturdy young lady of eighteen, the daughter of one of his natural-science professors at Kingston. Frieda was big, pallid and given to both bouts of tremendous enthusiasm and terrific sloughs of despond — at these latter times, a kind of bleak melancholy would descend over her parents' tranquil household like a low-pressure weather system blown in from the Great Lakes, oppressive and menacing. Frieda's looks were as changeable as her moods: her milk white skin would be clear as a field of fresh snow one moment, then, at the slightest provocation, she would break out in stupendous hives. She also tended towards random puffiness and was exceptionally susceptible to pink eye.

The marriage was scheduled for the autumn of 1910, by which time it was hoped that Frieda would have passed her Royal Conservatory exams, a goal that thus far had eluded her, owing to an apparently inherent inability to beat time.

According to the directive he received from the Bureau of Mines, George was to follow mining-claim lines north of the Porcupine; he was advised not only to survey the terrain, but also to report with reference to means of access, topography, wildlife and vegetation.

George took the Canadian Pacific to Mattagami, a little settlement about seventy miles west of Sudbury, purchased a cottonwood canoe and paddled it down the Spanish to the Mattagami River and down the Mattagami to Porcupine Lake. This lake formed the centre from which the gold camp, which extended over several small settlements, radiated. He was to set up headquarters at the new town of Golden City, on the northeast shore of the lake, as it boasted a dual post and telegraph office.

He took with him a small tent, rope, twine, wire, an axe, brush hooks, a spade, a grindstone, a whetstone, a scythe, packstraps, survey pickets, chain pins, a standard Gunter's Chain (one hundred links, or sixty-six feet, long), scribing irons, and an instrument box containing a Dollard sextant with a ten-inch radius, an artificial horizon, a thermometer, a solar compass accurate within two minutes, a micrometer and two aneroid barometers. George's telescope — or brasses, as surveyors named this instrument — was a small, portable astronomical transit that he could mount on a tree stump. In a battered leather portfolio he carried compiled mathematical tables, a half a dozen blank journals, two pens, a box of pencils and a supply of black ink. He also carried a duffel bag with a change of uniform and, neatly folded and tucked away in their own case, the Union Jack and the red-and-white pennant of the Geological Survey. These he was instructed to fly so that anyone encountering him in the bush might recognize that he was a government surveyor working in an official capacity.

"Suspected claim-jumpers have been known to meet with mischief in the wild, unruly North," his supervisor had advised him. "Even to disappear entirely."

Golden City was little more than a main street dug out of thick, fecund mud and haphazardly lined with shanties in various states of construction or disrepair. In addition to the post and telegraph office (housed in the trading post), there were a couple of outhouses (one for hire), a saddler's, a structure that resembled a woodpile but was in fact a public house, and a two-storey log rooming house run by Mrs. Flowers.

Mrs. Flowers was a bulky woman of indeterminate middle age who wore a fringed buckskin coat and Wellingtons year-round. She rented out eight rooms to prospectors and others trafficking in the bush. Sometimes she grubstaked them. George, however, earned forty-five dollars a month, and so paid the full board of sixty cents a day. "It would cost you less if you shared a bed," Mrs. Flowers advised him. "Course, then there's lice to worry about."

Mrs. Flowers kept a cow called Betty, famous for her omnivorous nature. "Once," Mrs. Flowers told George, "she ate a whole pile of socks I was fixing to darn. Another time she ate a Bible."

In anticipation of future settlement and to facilitate the surveyance of a large tract of heavily timbered terrain, a grid had been laid over the area. This was to parcel it up into discrete chunks or townships, which were then named after various men in the bureau and their friends: Blackstock, Childerhose, Wark, Zavitz. Eighty in all. The term "township" was somewhat misleading in that there were, in fact, no towns. This was because there were, in fact, no people. Outside of the little settlements of Golden City, Pottsville, South Porcupine and Aura Lake, and the occasional trapper working his lines in isolation or an Ojibwa fishing camp made up of two or three families and pitched by a lake, the entire country was untrammelled, unexplored bush.

George's experience bore this out. Since leaving Golden City one morning two weeks earlier to survey the northernmost townships of Moberly, Thorburn, Reid, Carnegie, Prosser, Tully and Little, he had seen a mother bear and her cubs, a whole score of deer, a fox, some martens, a colony of beavers, three wolves ravening what looked to be a caribou . . . but no human beings.

Then he saw her.

But first he saw the moose.

It was just before sunrise, and he was paddling down the snaking, green Buskegau River, heading east towards Frederick House Lake. The tops of the trees were bathed in mist the colour of goose down. The air was thick, soft and cool. It was very quiet; the birds had not yet begun to sing, and he could hear the river run.

Suddenly, he heard a crashing sound in the bush. Moments later, a massive bull moose lumbered out of the forest and stood winking at him from the bank, a distance of some fifteen feet. Its big, bony face looked forlorn, its hide moth-eaten and patchy.

George had never observed a moose at such close proximity. Quickly, he manoeuvred the canoe into some bulrushes along the opposite bank and, laying his paddle across his lap, leaned forward eagerly to watch the huge beast.

The moose observed all this activity on the geologist's part with a sorrowful and somewhat puzzled expression, then it waggled its unwieldy antlers. The gesture did not appear hostile so much as it seemed to be an attempt on the part of the animal to shake off a ridiculous oversized party hat that had somehow become affixed to its head. Moose shed their antlers after the fall rut, George knew. He wondered if they itched.

After the moose was done shaking its antlers, it delicately picked its way to the water's edge and, stretching out its neck, began to munch on the yellow water lilies that grew there with its big, square herbivore teeth, its lips fumbling about the coarse stalks. Throughout all this, its gaze remained riveted on George.

Carefully, so as not to startle the animal, George extracted a notebook and a pencil from the breast pocket of his khaki jacket and set them on his knee. "First moose I've seen up close," he wrote in his precise hand, then he glanced to either side of him. "Wild plum on river's bank," he continued, "in full bloom."

A red-winged blackbird dropped down on a bulrush a few feet from where the canoe drifted and began to scream her territory at George. *Mine! Mine!* Overhead, a black crow cackled a raucous alarm. *Macoun! Macoun!* as if the invader was a known entity whose terrible arrival had long been anticipated.

"Just before dawn. Birds waking up. Crow. Red-winged

blackbird," George concluded, closing the notebook and setting it back on his knee. With his chin resting on his hand, he regarded the moose. The moose regarded him back, munching water lilies. In this way, ten minutes passed, then twenty. George's eyes drifted shut and his head dropped to one side; he slumped forward. The slight current rocked the canoe idly, like a weary mother tips a cradle, back and forth, back and forth.

Strata . . . Data . . . Strata . . . Data . . . The words alternated in his mind: one, then the other. Like the ticktocking of Frieda's metronome. He was trying to come up with a rhyme for strata that wasn't data. How about matter or evolutionary ladder? George had written poetry since his undergraduate days at Kingston, employing geological metaphors for the most part, as these were the terms and concepts with which he was most familiar. Once, he had read out loud to Frieda several verses of a dandy one on synclinal folds and anticlinal hollows. It was a more or less a love sonnet. His fiancée had responded by looking stunned — not the response he had hoped for. Later, she explained that she had been thinking of something else.

A gauzy mist swirled around the reeds, trailed disembodied cloud fingers over the dark green water, bathed his face in coolness. Suddenly, there was the sound of branches snapping and vegetation being crunched underfoot. Startled, George opened his eyes. The moose had finished its meal and was clambering up the bank and into the bush, its big head lolling from side to side, its tail twitching.

"What?" George sputtered, half-starting from his seat. His action sent the notebook flying. He dove for it, catching it just before it pitched over the side into the river and jerking it up over his head, for the moment he lunged, he had felt the canoe tip. A second later, it rolled over, tumbling George into the waist-high water.

A gasp of muffled laughter.

George froze, still holding the notebook aloft, then slowly he twisted around and looked back over his shoulder in the direction from which the sound had come. He could just make out, half-hidden in the shadow of the wild plums, a slender form, a girl perhaps or a small woman, clothed in something white, a shift of some kind that ended mid-calf. "Hello?" he ventured.

The figure retreated a step and half-turned, as if to run away.

"Wait!" said George. "Don't go. Please. You needn't be afraid of me." He replaced the notebook in his breast pocket and buttoned it closed. "My journal," he explained. "Can't lose that! Very important. I'm a geologist, you see. We take a lot of notes. Oh, I say! Maybe you're French. A lot of Frenchmen in these parts. *Bonjour, mademoiselle! Comment allez-vous?*"

She turned towards him. "*Bonjour,*" she replied in a small voice, scarcely audible.

"Well, then!" George beamed. "That's dandy! The only problem is that I don't speak French. Not apart from *bonjour* and *au revoir*, that is. I speak German. German is the language of science, and I . . . well, I'm a scientist, you see."

She said nothing, only looked at him with big, round eyes of some indescribable colour.

"I know I'm talking an awful lot, but it's been two weeks since I've seen another human being. . . . Oh! Don't be frightened now," he cautioned her, "but I'm wet, you see. How do you say it? *Humide?* I'm just going to right this canoe and come ashore so I can dry off." He flipped the canoe over and pushed it up onto the riverbank. Then he plucked the oilskin bag that held his instruments from the river's weedy bottom and clambered ashore. As if there were some requisite distance that had to be maintained between them, she retreated a few steps backwards into the bush as he came forward.

"Thank goodness for oilskin," he said, setting the bag on the ground and opening it. "Lucky for me, most of my gear is at base camp." He hunkered down and removed his instruments from the bag, setting them on the grass to dry.

"What are these?" She took a tentative step forward, pushing a bough of plum out of the way as she did and leaning forward to get a better look at the implements.

"You speak English!" he exclaimed

"Papa was English; Maman, she spoke French," she answered softly. "But these shiny things . . . How do you call them? They are very pretty."

"Well, this is what's called a Dollard sextant." George showed her the sextant. "And this is an artificial horizon. I'm doing a survey, you see."

She stared at him quizzically for a moment, then cocked her head to one side. "What?" she asked.

"A geological survey for the Bureau of Mines."

She frowned, as though still confused.

"For making a map," he continued.

"Oh," she said. "And what is a . . . How did you call it?"

"A map. It's a sort of picture of a place," George explained. "This country around here. Of the rivers and the lakes and how far it is from one place to the other."

"Ah!" she exclaimed.

"But where do you live?" George asked.

"Over there," she replied. Turning, she pointed in a southeasterly direction.

"Far?" George asked.

"Not far," she replied. "On the Lake."

"What lake?" George reached for his notebook.

"The Lake," she answered.

"I mean, what is it called? This lake?"

"The Lake," she articulated carefully, as though he might be hard of hearing. "But I must go now."

"No!" cried George. "I mean, can't you wait a minute?"

"No," she said. "*Au revoir, monsieur!*"

She turned on her heel then and, pushing the plum boughs out of her way, darted into the forest. For a moment, he could discern a glint of her white dress as she moved between the trees, then nothing. She was gone.

George sat down heavily on the bank and stared hard at the river. As long as she had been standing opposite him, it had been all he could do not to stare at her, or for that matter, to speak coherently. Yet now, moments after she had gone, he found that he could not recall a single feature of her face or an aspect of her figure — how young or old she was, what the colour of her hair was, whether her complexion was pale or swarthy. Nothing save that she had been dressed in white and was the most beautiful woman he had ever seen . . . if, indeed, he had seen her and she was not some hallucination born of his extended isolation or an angel tumbled into this remote northern place by some celestial accident.

Starting to his feet and taking up his instruments, he began to determine his coordinates. How many degrees north and west. The place where first he had seen her.

July 17, 1910

Dearest Frieda,

 I can't imagine that you would like this God-forsaken place. It is very rough and fraught with all sorts of dangers. Just yesterday, I came upon a hole in which one hundred garter snakes lay tangled in one wriggling mass as big as a medicine ball — a repulsive sight that I'm sure would have made you scream and faint — and the blackflies are now in full season. I cannot begin to describe the horror of the blackfly. Every inch of my body that is not covered by clothing is slavered with fly dope — a more evil smell I can't imagine — and still the demons crawl and bite! Well, I know how much you hate snakes and flies. It's no place for women, that's for sure, so don't even think about coming, as you suggested in your last letter. In fact, the only woman I have met so far up here is Mrs. Flowers, who runs the rooming house, and she smokes cigars.

 I am glad to hear that the Schubert is going well, but please don't trouble yourself so much on account of the meter. If you would only relax a little, the ringing in your ears might abate and then you could hear the metronome more clearly.

 Fondest regards,
 George

Telling himself that he must double-check his earlier coordinates — he had made his calculations at dawn, after all, without reference to any celestial body — George made his way back to the Buskegau in late July. In order to arrive at a more accurate reading, he first had to determine his astronomic meridian, which, in turn, meant that he had to observe the elongation of Polaris. This could be done only at night, when the star was visible. Accordingly, he set up a station in a little clearing downstream from the grove of wild plums in which he had first encountered the woman or sprite — he was not entirely convinced that he had not imagined their conversation. The spot boasted a stump on which to set up his transit and a stretch of flat, dry ground carpeted with fragrant jack pine needles on which to pitch his tent. He struck camp and settled down to wait for nightfall.

At a quarter past eight, just as he was transcribing the last of the day's field notes into his journal, he heard a laboured, dragging sound such as a predator, perhaps a wolf, might make dragging prey to its lair. Standing carefully, so as to make no sound, he reached for his rifle. Just as his fingers closed around the stock of the gun, he saw a lone figure standing in the shadows. It was the woman. She was wearing a man's plaid shirt and denim overalls much too large for her. Her hair hung loose and tangled around her face. She was breathing heavily, as if from some great exertion. George could see her chest rise and fall beneath the plaid shirt. He could just make out a travois of some kind that she was dragging. It was loaded down with bundles whose shape was difficult to determine in the half-light of dusk.

"Hello!" he exclaimed. "Well, golly! So you're real, after all!" He leaned the rifle against a jack pine.

She swallowed and glanced uncertainly at him. "Is it you, then?" she asked, her voice subdued, strangely ragged. She seemed dazed, unsteady on her feet. Her hands rose to her face, clawed the hair away from her eyes. "You came back, then."

He could see that her face was smudged with what looked like soot from a fire and streaked . . . From what? From tears? "Come to check my coordinates," he explained, suddenly solicitous. "But what is that you're dragging? It looks pretty heavy. Maybe I could help you." He pointed. "My canoe is right over there."

She glanced at the travois' contents and then back to him. Her eyes were large and grey, like glass, empty of expression. "My children," she said flatly. "My children are in the travois."

"Children!" George exclaimed, surprised. He had not reckoned on her having children. She scarcely looked old enough, or at any rate, he could not tell how old she looked. "Well," he stammered. "Children! How many?"

"Two," she replied. "There are two."

"A boy and a girl?" George asked.

She nodded, then bowed her head and half-turned away, covering her face with her hands.

"What? What is it?" George demanded. Striding over to her, he took her by the shoulder.

"Dead!" she cried. "They are dead!"

"What?" He fell back a step.

"They are dead," she repeated. Then, her words coming in a rush, she said, "They died last night. Both of them. First the boy, then the girl. Pamphile died night before last. Pamphile was my husband. I buried him yesterday. Tonight

I bury them. There is a good burying place . . . up there."
She pointed to a spar of high ground upriver — it was
about sixty feet distant and visible from the clearing. "I
could not drag Pamphile so far, but they are little, not so
heavy as Pamphile. I buried him near the shed. All night
long, the wolves came . . . the ravens. I did not want to hear
them come for my children too."

George dropped to his haunches and peered into the
travois: two oblong bundles, each about three feet long,
wrapped in faded pink flannelette. He reached out one
hand to touch the bundle nearest him, felt a density that
leaked cold through the worn cloth, as if the flannelette
encased stones. A shovel, still clumped with damp earth,
presumably from her last excavation, was lashed to the
poles with Gillings twine. "What . . . what happened?" he
whispered.

"Spots, fever," she explained. "Their eyes rolled back
into their heads. Later I realized that they were dead. Gone.
That they did not breathe. I don't know what the illness is
. . . if it has a name. All three of them . . . two days was all it
took." She stumbled forward as if she might fall, then
caught herself, swaying. In the dim light she looked pale,
ghastly, as though the blood had been drained from her.
There were mauve circles, the colour of a bruise, smudged
under her eyes — these were almost too large for her heart-
shaped face, and they had turned the transparent grey
colour of moonstones. George's eyes caught on them like a
drifting leaf will catch on a twig, and then hung there for a
moment, pierced, pinioned.

Then he realized with a start: the woman can't have
slept for the past thirty-six hours. She must be exhausted,

barely able to stand. He rose quickly from the travois and, stepping forward, took her forearm in one hand and her shoulder in the other. "Here," he said gently, urgently, his lips close to her ear as he steadied her with his hands. "You're not to worry now. I will help you."

"Yes," the woman agreed, clinging to him. "Yes, please. That would be good. You are very kind."

Releasing her, he stepped out in front of the travois and, grasping the two poles behind him, started to drag the sledge up the little rise. It was heavy — much heavier than he would have thought possible, given the age of the children, which he reckoned by the length of the bundles to be no more than four or five years. The woman stumbled along behind him, reaching out now and again to catch at the back of his belt to steady herself. He had no idea how she could have dragged such a heavy object any distance at all — the top of her head barely reached his collarbone and she appeared very slight beneath what he thought must be her husband's clothes.

When they reached the top of the rise, he set the travois down and, after untying the twine that held the shovel in place, dug two shallow graves in the rocky soil. Then he excused himself and returned to his campsite for his oil lamp, for the sun had set and it had grown quite dark while he was digging. When he returned, the two pink bundles lay tucked into the earth as if in two narrow beds. The woman knelt, arranging the flannelette as though the shrouds were bedclothes, tucking the fabric in here and smoothing it there.

"You should have waited," George protested. "I would have done that for you."

"I am putting them to bed for the last time," she said. "These are my children. I will have no more. *Padre, filie et spiritu sancti*." She leaned over the little bodies, making the sign over the cross over each. "*Padre, filie et spiritu sancti*." Then she stood, brushing the soil from her knees. "Quickly," she told George. "We must cover them up."

George shovelled earth over the flannel bundles and, at the woman's insistence and with her frenzied help, collected big stones and heaped them upon the graves.

"I cannot bear to find their bones strewn about," she explained as she crouched, fitting the stones more tightly into place. "Once my father found an old woman's head, which an animal had torn from her body and dragged away. He threw it deep into the bush only to have it turn up in a different place. It was a terrible-looking thing, its eyes gouged out, the flesh laid bare and half-eaten off the bone. Stinking. The third time he found it, he was going to throw it in the lake, but Mother said, 'No, we must fish in that lake,' and so he buried it instead."

When they had finished, George offered to pack up his gear and tent and take the woman anywhere she wished to go. "Perhaps you'll want to be with your family," he suggested.

She shook her head. "My family is dead. I have no family," she said.

"You won't want to be alone," he advised her. "I'll take you down to Golden City and put you up at Mrs. Flowers's. I'll pay for your room and board until you can get yourself settled."

She shook her head again. "No," she said, "I live by the lake. I have always lived by the lake. Why should I leave?"

"Well, then," said George, not knowing what to do — for surely chivalry demanded that he take some action to assure her safety and well-being. "I'll take you home. I'll camp outside your door, make sure you are all right. Just for tonight."

"No need. I have lived alone before. After Papa died. Before Pamphile. I can do so again." She held out her hand to him and he took it eagerly. Her slender fingers were cool, her hand felt boneless.

"At least tell me your name," George urged her.

"Marguerite," she replied. "My parents called me Marguerite."

"And I'm George. George Macoun."

"Thank you for helping me bury my children, George Macoun. You have been very kind." She withdrew her hand from his grasp and, turning, bent down to pick up the shovel.

"No, let me do that," George insisted.

"It is not necessary," she said, swinging the shovel over her shoulder.

"What about the sledge?" he asked.

"Some poles lashed together. I do not want it," she said. "Goodbye, George Macoun!" She started off into the thick forest.

"Marguerite, wait! You're going the wrong way!" George cried. "My camp is that way. West!"

"I'm taking a shortcut," she called over her shoulder as she continued to make her way through the bush, not looking back.

"No! Really! I insist!" cried George, starting after her. "I'll make you some tea! Wait up!"

"Don't follow me, George Macoun!" she called. "I will be all right."

"But, Marguerite! What about wolves? What about bears?"

"Why should wolves or bears bother me?"

He could no longer see her. Then the forest swallowed even the sound of her footfalls.

August 3, 1910

Dear Frieda,

After several weeks in the region of Evelyn, I have come east again to the Tully township and the green, meandering Buskegau. It seems that my efforts to survey this little part of the world are doomed to frustration and failure, for the journal in which I had recorded my field notes for that region tumbled out of my packsack and into picturesque Ice Chest Lake of an evening as I was lazily paddling across its cool and tranquil waters. I fished about for twenty minutes and finally managed to dredge it up from the weedy bottom with my brush hook; it was, of course, a soggy and illegible wreck.

So it seems I will be an additional few weeks in the North. I am so very sorry, my dearest, but expect that you and your mother can continue to plan the wedding with the same energy and aplomb in my absence as you have all along. After all, what need for the humble George but to exist . . . and to be at the altar of St. Andrews at 11 a.m. sharp on October 4, of course! In the meantime, I'm sure you would agree that it would not do to disappoint the Bureau of Mines, which (rumours have it) will be increasing my salary to a princely fifty dollars a month if all goes well here in the Porcupine country.

Yours with the greatest of affection,
George

Three days later, George was tracking Marguerite south of his base camp when a thunderstorm blew up, driven from the southwest by strong, hot winds. It was going onto five o'clock in the afternoon when it arrived in the form of slanting rain, followed by big chunks of hail and thunderbolts so loud it sounded as though the granite shield beneath his feet was being split in two by a giant sledgehammer. The ground shook. The air was charged with electricity. George's instruments began to spark and buzz as though they had come to sudden, distraught life. The hair on his head and neck stood on end. He could feel the hairs tugging at their follicles. A jagged bolt of lightning struck a jack pine not twenty feet from where he had sought shelter under a felled tree. There was an acrid smell of frying pine sap and sulphur. The jack pine sizzled like a sparkler, then burst into hot, orange flame.

It was then that he saw her, a dark figure silhouetted against the burning jack pine, her head and shoulders covered by a blanket as she moved towards him through the thick brush. "Here," she cried, extending her arm to offer him shelter under the blanket. "My house is nearby."

He scrambled to his feet, stooped to come under the blanket. "But how did you know I was here?" he asked.

"You've been here for days," she replied. "Do you think I've haven't known?"

She led him down a rooty path to a trapper's rough cabin huddled in a grove of tall birches beside a small lake, round as a cauldron. The storm lashed the lake; its waters churned and boiled. Through the hard, driving rain the sentinel birches wavered like pale, elongated ghosts guarding the pile of moss-chinked logs; their papery leaves fluttered lightly, like the wings of a hundred little birds. Shoving open the heavy, sticking door, she pushed him inside, tossed the wet blanket over a chair back and, moving to a battered table, bent over to light the coal-oil lamp.

The wick caught the flame and held it; a moment later, a portion of the room ballooned into a soft pool of yellow light. George blinked to adjust his vision, then glanced around him. The peeled log walls had been hewn and recently whitewashed. One corner was completely taken up with a large iron bedstead, on which a feather tick lay; this was covered with a faded patchwork quilt. In the other corner squatted an oval tin stove, dented and shiny. The floor was made up of uneven planks cut from slivery white pine and strewn, here and there, with rag rugs in muted blues and greens. A chipped blue vase on the table beside the lamp held a spray of magenta heather. He inhaled deeply. The cabin smelled of resin, faintly of woodsmoke

and of something else besides, a composite of odours —
lavender, camomile, witch hazel and borage.

Marguerite pulled out a rickety three-legged stool for
him, handed him a dry Hudson's Bay blanket to wrap himself in and set the kettle on the stove for tea, which she gave
to him in a blue granite chip mug. It was not ordinary tea
but some tisane decocted from bark or a root tasting faintly
of licorice.

"I have no English tea," she explained. "It is all gone.
Sometimes Pamphile would buy it from the trader when he
sold his furs. Twinings. Not me. I have never been to town."

"Would you like to go?" George asked.

"Oh, no!" replied Marguerite, shuddering.

Gingerly, George sipped the hot, strong fluid and watched
her towel her hair dry. He could not tell what colour that hair
was even now by the light of the coal-oil lamp . . . or even its
length. Like her eyes, it seemed almost colourless, the shade of
greyish dun that woodsmoke is or haze, and it not so much
fell from her head as emanated from it, like a mist at dawn that
clings to the body of the river that begets it.

The cloth of her wet shift clung here and there to her
slender body as she lifted her arms and turned a little this
way and that to accomplish the towelling. George looked at
her hungrily, then, realizing what he was doing, he averted
his glance. You are a gentleman, George Macoun, he
reminded himself, an alumnus of Queen's University and
engaged to be married in but a few months' time to . . . Who
was he marrying? Frantically, he poked around in his brain
until, a moment later, he had uprooted the name: Frieda! Yes,
of course! He was marrying Frieda Eckert.

Frieda?

"What is the matter, George?" Marguerite asked. "You look so strange."

George swallowed. "You said you had been watching me."

Marguerite shrugged. "Yes," she replied.

"Why?" George asked.

The woman tossed the towel over the back of a chair and pushed her damp hair from her face. She did not answer for a moment. Then she said, "In the winter there are Pamphile's traplines to work, but in the summer there's not much to do." She pointed to a fishing pole that leaned against the door. "Now and then I fish. There are sauger in the lake and walleye. Do you like to fish, George Macoun?"

But George would not be diverted. "Why did you keep yourself hidden, Marguerite?" he asked. "Did you think I wouldn't want to see you? I . . . I wanted to see you. Very much. Well, what I mean is that I was worried about you. Concerned, I mean."

"Concerned?" she repeated.

"A woman alone . . . a pretty one . . ." George faltered. Surely the concept of female helplessness was too obvious to require an explanation!

"Oh! But I was alone for many years after Papa died," she reassured him. "Five or six, at least. Let's see. Maman turned to dust when I was just gone eight and Papa a few years later. He died of gangrene. His right leg, all the way to the groin. In the end, I had to shoot him. Later, Pamphile —

George spat a mouthful of tea into his lap. "What?" he blurted out.

"Pardon?" she inquired, blinking at him.

"You shot," George sputtered, "your father?"

"He was suffering," she said softly. "You wouldn't believe

the screaming . . . or the stench, to be quite honest! So, you see, you needn't be concerned for me, George. I am good at taking care of myself."

George wiped his mouth with the back of his hand and mopped at his lap with a frayed corner of the scratchy blanket. "I suppose," he admitted ruefully. He was trying to imagine Frieda, whom a metronome could reduce to tears and shrieks, taking aim at a howling, reeking Dr. Eckert with the professor's pearl-handled derringer. Dr. Eckert kept just such a gun in his desk drawer — "In case a thief bent upon stealing my prize butterfly collection should break into my office," the professor had explained. George found the image a difficult one to conjure.

"Anyway," Marguerite continued, "I was curious to see if you could find me. I am hard to find, it seems."

"Very hard," George agreed.

"So I found you instead. Because, in truth, you were not so hard to find, and besides, it was enough that you should have looked for me in the first place."

George's heart snagged on her words as if on a thorn, and then hung from them, beating like a wounded thing that struggles and cannot tear itself free. Blood roared in his ears, making it difficult for him to hear, to think. "Enough for what?" he managed to whisper. "What are we talking about?"

"I am supposed to stay right here," Marguerite explained. "By the Lake. I am not supposed to go across the river or beyond the grove of birches to the west or the vale of the jack pines to the east. I may go no farther south than an hour's walk."

"What do you mean 'not supposed to,' 'can't go'?" George asked. "Of course you can go!"

"No," insisted Marguerite firmly. "I cannot. I am different from you, George. Different from Papa and Pamphile, too. I am like my mother. Papa tried to take her across the river when she was ill with fever. She told him not to move her, but he wouldn't listen. Then she became feverish and no longer understood what was being said to her. It was January and very cold. Papa wrapped her up in his warmest furs and laid her in the toboggan. He hitched up the dogs, calling to me to wait and to stay inside no matter what. Later that night he returned. No sooner had they crossed the ice on the river than Maman had shivered away into a handful of white dust that the wind blew everywhere. Papa said he had never seen anything like it. She simply disintegrated. She always told him something terrible would happen were she to leave the Lake — that was what her own mother had told her — but she was never sure what that thing was. After that, Papa made sure I understood that I could never leave. And I made sure Pamphile knew it. You see, Papa found Maman here at the Lake the way her papa had found her maman. Just as Pamphile found me . . . just as you found me. As far as I know, that is the way it always has been."

"But it's a fairy story you've just told me," George objected. "Surely you can't believe it. For one thing, the French came into this country at the very earliest two hundred years ago. That's hardly forever."

Marguerite shrugged. "I don't know. Perhaps we were not French."

George stared at her, at her creamy, pale skin, her haze of colourless hair, her transparent eyes. "What do you mean 'not French'?" he whispered.

She did not answer. Instead, she tugged the mug of tea

from his hands and set it on the table. He stood, as if she had drawn him to his feet by taking away the cup, and turned to leave. For surely he must leave — and quickly, he told himself. His thinking was all muddled and there was . . .

Marguerite caught him by the sleeve of his shirt. "Don't go!" she pleaded, her voice low, as warm as fur.

There was someone called Frieda . . .

Reluctantly, inexorably, George turned to Marguerite, and as he did, he found himself hurled off his feet and spun into a wild vortex in which there was no sound, no footing to be found, but only hands and twining arms and hair as soft as mist and warm mouths.

George stayed at the little lake in the woods for a fortnight. Then he returned to Mrs. Flowers's in Golden City in preparation for his journey to Kingston. The morning before he was to portage out, however, he wrote his fiancée another letter.

August 21, 1910

Darling Frieda,

The most ridiculous news imaginable! I begin to think my expedition to this place has been cursed by those Greek and Roman gods that so oft find their way into our stimulating literary discussions. No sooner had I completed my field notes for the

Tully township and journeyed to Golden City in joyful and expectant anticipation of returning to you, my beloved, than my journal was eaten by Mrs. Flowers's ridiculous cow! The greedy creature left only the spine! That means that I must return yet again to the bush, as I cannot show my face at the bureau without the information I was sent to collect. Would you mind dreadfully if we were to postpone the wedding just one week? I shall endeavour to fulfil my task as quickly as possible, God and weather permitting — not to mention voracious ruminants! — so that I may return to you and put an end to this long separation.

Sincerely,
Your adoring George

For, by this time, George had learned to lie.

After posting the letter, George went out back of the rooming house to Mrs. Flowers's cow shed and held out his journal for Old Betty to eat.

George Dewey Macoun returned to Kingston from Northern Ontario in the late fall of 1910 and married Frieda Eckert on October 22 of that year. Several months later, the new Mrs. Macoun failed her Royal Conservatory exams for the third time. By then, however, she was carrying the first of their four children and was too overwhelmed by nausea to do more than take to her bed. There she lay moaning, with a damp towel folded over her pale and tremendous forehead and a bucket strategically placed by the head of her bed.

George was not on hand when the second George Macoun, his namesake, was born. He had gone north again for the purpose of performing more precise observations regarding longitude. He explained the process to Frieda once. Something to do with exact local time and when the moon crosses the meridian of the observation plane, whatever that meant! To tell the truth, Frieda had been only half-listening to her husband, who could be quite pedantic when he started in on his stream gauging and his catchment delineation. "Such an odd, dusty duck! Just like Father with his bugs!" said Frieda, laughing.

When George went north, he always stayed at Mrs. Flowers's. At least, that was the address to which Frieda posted her bright, chatty letters, full of news about herself and their children. Often he didn't reply to those letters for weeks. But he was so frequently in the field and returned to town only for supplies or to file reports.

After years of exacting and meticulous fieldwork, George produced an admirable rendering of the 1,239 square miles that would later become incorporated as the City of Timmins, the largest municipality, in terms of land mass, in all of Canada. He mapped its streams, its rivers, its many little and big lakes and all the islands in them. There was one lake, however, that he failed to include on his map.

Shortly before the birth of his fourth child, George Macoun went north again. Because there had been problems with the printer regarding the second edition of his map, he had been unable to leave Southern Ontario for more than six months. He had never been away from the Porcupine for so long, not since he had first begun going north more than a decade earlier.

"The ministry wants me to suggest some potential reservoir sites," he explained to Frieda. "I'll need to establish some benchmarks."

When he arrived at the little cabin by the uncharted lake, all was still. The cabin had a derelict quality, as though it had been abandoned for a season. The roof sagged and the logs were dark with rot, while the woodpile on the porch was tumbled, sticks here and there as though an animal had been rooting through them. Strangely, the foundation of the cabin was still banked with clay; Marguerite always removed the clay after the thaw to let the logs breathe, but here it was well into June.

George's heart squeezed into a tight fist. "Marguerite!" he called hoarsely.

There was no reply.

The cabin door was ajar. Flinging it open, George glanced quickly about the dusky room. It looked as it always did — the chairs and table and bed in their accustomed places, the rag rugs placed just so. However, it smelled different. Empty. He stepped into the room, his heart turning over heavily in his chest like a punctured tire. She had left him a note on the table, one corner of it weighted down by the coal-oil lamp:

Dear George,

You have been gone so long. Months and months. I expected you before the thaw, yet that has long since passed. So I have decided to go looking for you. I think perhaps you are right and I will not turn to dust if I cross the river. We shall see . . .

Marguerite

That night, George pitched his tent beside the Lake and watched the loons run maniacally along the surface of the water to gain the necessary speed for flight. Year after year, they returned to this point on a map that did not exist on paper but was nevertheless etched deep into their hearts. Loons mate for life, Marguerite had told him.

Behind him the cabin burned. There was no wind that night, so the fire burned straight up. He could feel its heat spread across his back like the palm of a big hand. Now and then, there was a loud crack as the cone of a jack pine, pried open by the heat, burst, scattering its seeds.

Before he had poured coal oil over the cabin's contents and ignited it with a match from the tin box he kept in his kit, George had climbed up to the ridge where he and Marguerite had buried her children so many years before. One at a time, he removed the rocks that still covered the shallow graves. In truth, he had long wondered if he had not buried rocks or some other thing that night, for the little bodies had seemed too heavy, too stone cold for children and there was much about Marguerite he did not understand. The pink flannelette that had served the little bodies as shrouds had long since rotted into the soil, leaving it tinged with faint colour. In each grave he found not stones or bones but this: an elongated heap of snow white dust stretched into the shape of a child.

George asked Frieda if he could name their fourth child. Frieda found this mildly peculiar. "He showed absolutely no interest in naming the first three," she told her euchre club. "It was all up to me. Well, you know George. Nose in his notes if he's not in the field. But the name he chose! My dears! Outlandish! French, you know. Marguerite. I call her Margie, of course, but no nicknames for George. He always calls her by her full name. And how he dotes on that child, when, truth be told, he never paid one bit of attention to little George or Donald or Evelyn. The first thing he did after she was born was name a lake in Northern Ontario after her. A little glacial lake he had only just discovered: Lake Marguerite. How Evelyn carried on. Whinging and weeping. Where's my lake, Daddy? she wanted to know, and rightly so, if you ask me. And then, to top it all off, he buys all the land around the lake and builds a cottage and a boathouse, and that's why I have to miss Edna's Dominion Day tea — because every summer without fail the whole Macoun family has to train up to Lake Marguerite and catch sauger and walleye and be eaten alive by those appalling flies!"

"Marguerite!" gasped George, clutching at his daughter's plump hand. The hospital room was dark and shadowy, scarcely there at all. A millimetre above the white, glowing bed, the old geologist floated, not quite in contact with the sheets, suspended. "So you're still here, my dearest! Not gone? Not turned to dust?"

"Not yet, Daddy," Margie replied wanly. "Soon."

"I've been having the strangest dreams!" George told her. "I . . . I found you in the bush, and you were young and beautiful but so strange. And there were two children and a cabin. I never saw the children. For years, I —"

"Shhh!" Margie advised him, withdrawing her cool, fleshy hand from his feverish one and laying it on his steaming forehead instead. "Try to rest, Dad. They've got you on a morphine drip. It's no wonder your dreams are strange."

THE HEIFER

The heifer was a pretty brindle, white with flecks of red and black and grey. She was dainty, with ears that flickered and eyes like wavering, dark jelly. An intelligent-seeming heifer, sweet-smelling like grass.

"I shall name her Olga," Aina told her new husband — this was after her little sister back in Finland, Olga Lappi, whom she would never see again now that she had come all the way to New Ontario to marry Uwe Pahakka. "Truly, I have never before seen so beautiful a cow," she swore, stroking the heifer's sides, where the short hair felt like silk.

Uwe beamed. He knew that this was a fine compliment,

coming from a girl whose family owned a dairy farm. "I think she looks like you," he commented.

"Do you really?" Aina asked, shy and pleased.

Uwe had come out to Canada four years ago from Finland, leaving Aina behind. She was only fourteen at the time, and her parents said that she could follow her young suitor only when he had legal title to a farm, the documents to prove it and money for her passage. They had their reasons for these strictures. Uwe's father had been feckless and his mother had drifted off into a kind of untidy madness later in her life. "The Pahakkas are not good stock," her father had advised his protesting daughter.

The Lappis thought that they had heard the last of Uwe when he disappeared into that great hole in the world that was sucking up all the young men, North America. Surely such a disorganized, unsatisfactory boy, so given to momentary, riotous enthusiasms and sudden, prolonged bouts of melancholy, could not succeed in making a life for himself in such a hard, new place as Canada.

Indeed, Aina did not hear from her lover but twice in the four years that elapsed between his departure and the arrival of the letter requesting her hand in marriage. In his first letter, dated six months after his departure, he wrote that he had decided to go round the Horn of South America in order to make his fortune prospecting gold in the Yukon. "Everybody is going," he told her. In his second letter, dated two months after the first, he advised his fiancée that he had changed his mind. "No need to go to the Klondike," he assured her. "There are plenty of rocks right here in Ontario."

In fact, Uwe, who was in Toronto at the time, working on a construction crew, had hopped the train north when silver was discovered near Mile 103 on the Temiskaming and Northern Ontario Railway and had managed, through sheer haphazardness, to stake several solid claims before the area filled up with prospectors. He sold the claims for a good price and, after talking to a Frenchman who wanted to sell his land and move back to Quebec, put the proceeds towards the purchase of a farm.

Accordingly, enclosed with the third letter, the one that arrived a full four years after his emigration, was another, written on the stationary of the Government of Ontario, testifying to the fact that Uwe Pahakka indeed held title to a farm located in the township of Cobalt, New Ontario. Also enclosed was a money order, to be used towards Aina's passage to the New World.

"We are very fortunate," Uwe wrote his fiancée. "The land is partially cleared and there is a house already."

When the letter arrived in their little village, tied with string because it was so fat, Aina had practically forgotten Uwe. After all, she had not heard from him in three years. Lately she had thought she might marry another boy — the sturdy, tow-headed son of a neighbouring farmer. He had courted her off and on for two years, furtively at first, then more openly as time passed and still Uwe did not write. There had been talk between the two fathers of ceding some pasturage as Aina's dowry. Both men felt that the deal was to their advantage.

However, the idea of leaving her family and her village and everything that was familiar to her to move to a new country where everything was not old like it was in Finland and eroded with scrubbing — this idea caught in the girl's imagination and grew and grew until it became so large that she was hard put to squeeze anything in alongside it. The notion of moving to Canada and marrying Uwe Pahakka filled her brain to bursting.

In place of the childish affection she had once felt for Uwe, a whole new love began to assemble itself out of bits and pieces and snatches of memory. Some of these memories were of things that had actually happened — wildflowers that he had one day picked for her and given her by the stone wall near her father's well, words of endearment he had actually spoken in her ear when nobody was looking. Others were of events that she wished had transpired, sentiments that she hoped he might one day express. Like a woman who has gone blind during her lover's absence, Aina attempted to remember Uwe by passing her fingers over the contours of a stranger's face, repeating to herself until she was sure of it, "Yes! It is! There can be no mistake! It must be! Surely it is my darling!"

In no time at all, Aina managed to conceive so great a passion for her former lover that it could not be denied, not even by fathers bent on swapping land for grandchildren. When old Lappi refused to allow Aina to travel to Canada to marry Uwe, and even threatened to return to him his money order by the next post, she fasted for two months until she had grown so frail that she could no longer rise from her bed without assistance or stand without fainting.

"It is clear that she is determined to starve herself to

death if you will not let her marry young Pahakka," observed Father Hongo, the village pastor. (Father Hongo frequently found it convenient to discern God's will in obstinacy and other forms of resistance.) "You had better let her go, or her blood will be on your hands."

It was only then that Aina's father finally agreed to allow the girl to depart for Canada. He did not want the death of his daughter on his conscience, and besides, there was little Olga coming onto sixteen. She might do very nicely for the neighbour's son in a year or two, if his father was still interested in that pasturage.

The victorious Aina travelled by boat to Montreal and by train to Toronto, where Uwe met her at Union Station. They were married on the following day, October 14, 1910, by a Finnish pastor who had been to seminary with Father Hongo and to whom the old minister had written, saying that this was a reasonably good thing, Aina marrying Uwe, though perhaps not so good as it might be.

Following the ceremony, the newlyweds climbed on board the new T&NO and, sixteen long hours later, disembarked at the new town of Cobalt, which at that time was little more than a collection of rough log shanties separated by charred stumps.

Uwe hired a two-seater democrat and a big plough horse from what passed for the livery shop, then laid in supplies at the general store — seven bags of flour; one hundred pounds of sugar; a fifty-pound tin of lard; a fifty-pound bag of salt; one case each of dried apples, peaches, apricots, raisins and currants; a bag each of rice and beans and potatoes; a wooden tub of corn syrup, with a spout for pouring; and a side of salt pork. "We won't go into town much once the snow comes," he advised her, cramming the provisions, with no little difficulty, into the back of the rickety two-seater. Then, climbing onto the seat beside Aina, he drove the ten miles to the farm down a raw red road that, where it was swale, was corduroyed with tamarack posts and chinked with moss, and where it wasn't, ran like a river of sticky mud a foot and a half deep.

"Road's better when it freezes," Uwe explained. "It will freeze soon." They had to stop twice to push the buggy several hundred feet to a tidier patch of ground.

As they drove through this new land of Canada, Aina sat straight and tall, observing how the forest pressed in to either side of the road with an attentiveness honed all the sharper for trepidation. The forest was dense, boreal, at once dark and light, pointed and tall. Cedar and poplar and whitewood and tamarack, spruce and balsam with a thick undergrowth of scrappy maple and willow and alder. From a cedar swamp nearby, a whippoorwill called plosively. In the clear, chill air of the northern autumn, the bird's cry sounded as round as a silvery bell.

Then, at length, there it was: the farm. Formerly the property of Gui Rancourt, now of Uwe Pahakka, it was a tarpaper shanty huddled down in a clearing around which a scattering of ragged outbuildings — a privy, a cowshed, a root house — gravitated like shaggy dancers move around a centre. Out back of the shack stretched a field of blackened stumps and, to the west, a ramshackle barn made of what appeared to be sticks lashed together.

"Do you like it?" Uwe asked proudly. He beamed. "I thought I'd build a sauna out back in the spring. There's a pond there — deep and cold. And you will have a milk

cow. I'm getting you one from a neighbour, but we thought
we'd wait until it was a few months older before separating
it from the herd. We can see it, though. I will take you there
tomorrow, when we return the hack. My wedding present
to you."

That was how Aina first learned of the heifer, and so she
had clapped her hands and laughed aloud and kissed her
new husband squarely on the mouth in spite of the fact that
the black shack looked squatting and evil to her and the
field beyond the barn baneful, like a cemetery of wooden
crosses burnt by a careless and disdainful enemy.

For the next three months, Aina waited for the day when
Uwe would lead the heifer across the dooryard to her. It
was difficult not to dwell on the subject, as the dainty,
sweet-eyed cow was all Uwe could think of to talk about
to his new wife . . . and all Aina had left to hope for now
that her dearest wish — to join her childhood sweetheart
in Canada and marry him — had apparently been granted.

For this reason, whenever a silence began to gape
between the two, like a chasm soundlessly riven through
the rock on which they stood and through which they
might plunge to a muffled doom; whenever they found
themselves standing in the middle of the tiny cabin (sixteen
by twenty feet), staring at one another with eyeballs burned
bald and raw from earlier eye wars and chimney smoke,
both poised to speak, both wondering if what was in their
hearts to say would somehow manage to smuggle itself out

in a packet of words so artfully arranged that, finally, the other would understand and forgive, and they could both walk away from each other and from this place once and for all; whenever Uwe felt that he must somehow atone for bringing Aina so far from her family to live alone with a man as simple and, well, uneventful as he in a little tarpaper shack in the middle of a frozen wilderness so glaringly white that it razed the corneas of a man's eye and so cold that it made of his fingers and his toes wood; or whenever he decided that he might snowshoe into Cobalt to the blind pig to lift a pint or two of that good Calgary Ale (a man's privilege!) and play a little blackjack (a fellow could go stir-crazy sitting in a shack all the long winter with nothing to do and only a sour-faced girl to keep him company!) — then it was that Uwe would go on and on about the heifer and what a beauty she was and how everything would be all right once the cow was on the farm: "She'll be a companion to you," he assured Aina. "You'll see!"

For by that time, it was clear that Uwe was not, nor could he ever be, a true companion to Aina.

From the time of their reunion and marriage in Toronto, and extending over November, December and January of that year, the love that had driven Aina to leave home and come to Canada to marry Uwe Pahakka began to dry up and blow away, like arid earth that no roots hold in place. The lover whom she had remembered had, of course, never really existed, and the man who was Uwe Pahakka proved no substitute for this exemplary phantom. Uwe was, upon closer scrutiny, not so handsome as she had recollected, nor, if the truth be told, handsome at all. Yes, he was tall — six foot three or four (he had to stoop when he was inside the shack or skin his pate on the log beams of the ceiling), but he was also ungainly. His pant legs were always too short, as were his sleeves, exposing big knobs of ankles and wrists. His hair was so blond as to be almost white, but it was thinning and clung to his skull in stray wisps. There was no centre to his pale eyes — this was disconcerting — and his teeth were spaced too far apart.

In addition, her husband reminded Aina of an old woman, rattling brittly on and on about nothing at all and given to endless repetition. When he became excited, he flushed a deep, turkey red and stammered, spraying saliva everywhere. Conversely, when his spirits were low or Aina had spoken sharply to him, he would lay down on the prickly, sharp-smelling mattress she had woven of balsam boughs, roll onto his side, face the wall and pull his knees up towards his chest, moaning softly. He would whimper like this for hours, until she was of a mind to beat him to death with a shovel.

Finally, Uwe was, in Aina's estimation, intolerably lazy. Though he had made good on the silver claims up around Mile 103, he might as well have washed his hands in the money they brought him, for all those dollar bills that they had fetched ran through his big, clumsy fingers just like water.

All these ponderings and ruminations came to a head one morning in early February, when Aina awoke, wincing into the cold grey light of a new day, with Uwe heavy and damp beside her in nubbly grey long johns, and thought to herself, tight-lipped, Aina Lappi, you have made a terrible mistake!

Then she lay very still beside her huge, unlovable husband and listened to the ice on the lake boom and the trees split with the cold — pop! —just like that, right down the middle! The wind spat and hissed inside the stove-pipe like an animal cornered in its burrow, determined to defend its young, and Aina began to plot her escape.

In mid-February, Aina, figuring that the heifer was now old enough to be moved to the farm, sent Uwe to fetch the cow from Old Farmer Lanthier.

"You'll see," he told Aina. "When Olga is here, you will have no more worries. You will be the happiest woman in New Ontario."

Unfortunately, there was a problem.

"Well, my friend," Old Farmer Lanthier told Uwe, "you could say that it's this way." Recognizing that Uwe's French was sparse, he spoke slowly and made elaborate gestures. "As for me, Old Farmer Lanthier, I live on this side of the river and you . . . you live on that." He pointed to here as being his feet and there as being somewhere to the west of his barn.

"Yes," Uwe agreed, nodding vigorously to indicate that he understood.

"To get from this side of the river to that, you must first cross the river," Lanthier continued, again pointing here and there and making an undulating motion with his hands to indicate waves.

Once more, Uwe was in agreement. "Yes, yes," he said.

"The ice," said Lanthier. *"La glace. Les vaches n'aiment pas la glace. Non. Non. Pas de tout."*

Uwe did not understand. "What? What?" he asked.

"Idiot!" declared Lanthier. "The cow will not cross glare ice. Trust me, my friend, she will walk on a mirror first!"

Dejected, Uwe returned home without the cow.

"It's no use," he said to his wife. "Lanthier says that Olga will not cross the glare ice."

"What?" Aina demanded. "The cow will not cross the ice? This man is trying to rob you! He is trying to cheat you! You have already paid him for the cow a long time ago, and now he will try to sell her again, to somebody else! Go back to him tomorrow and tell him that you want my cow now."

"But, Aina," Uwe protested. He did not want to go back to Lanthier's so soon. He was tired — Lanthier's farm was four miles east on the Cobalt road, which made the journey eight miles on snowshoes. Besides, the farmer had called him an idiot, and worse, he had treated him like one. Uwe took offence at that. "If Lanthier is right and Olga hates the ice, how am I to make her cross the river?"

"Of course he is right," snapped Aina impatiently. "Canadian cows are no different from Finnish cows. I don't know why I didn't think of it myself when you told me you were fetching her in February. But it is all right. I will make Olga boots!"

"Boots for a cow?" Uwe asked incredulously.

"Boots with spikes," Aina clarified. "That way, she will not be afraid to cross the ice."

"It is glare ice," Uwe reminded her.

"I know what I am talking about," insisted Aina.

The next day, Aina made four boots from three-ply leather that she studded with two-inch spikes. This task took her most of the day, as it was difficult to anticipate what size boot might fit Olga and how it could be lashed to her legs in such a way that the heifer would be unable to kick it off.

The following day, Aina rose an hour before dawn and made Uwe get up too so that they could snowshoe together to the Lanthier homestead. She was determined to fetch the cow home herself and to do so immediately so that Lanthier could not resell her. She was certain that was what the Frenchman intended.

Uwe complained bitterly the entire journey. "Old Farmer Lanthier will say that we are crazy, making boots for cows, and he will be right! I will be the laughing-stock of the entire township! Aina! Aina!" Long as his legs were, Uwe had trouble keeping up with his small, quick wife, who had made him carry in his packsack not only the makeshift cow boots, but also his own extra pair of hobnailed boots, for her to wear when the time came to lead Olga across the ice. "I will need traction," she had explained.

"What?' Aina retorted now. "You don't want to wait till spring, do you, when the ice melts and you must built a raft to float her across the torrent? Cows do not like water any more than they like ice!"

Uwe grumbled and yanked at his packsack. The big spikes hammered into the cow boots tore at the canvas from the inside and, despite his heavy Red River coat, clawed at the skin of his back.

"This I have to see!" said Old Farmer Lanthier when the Pahakkas had made their intentions known through what broken French Uwe, in his deep humiliation, could muster, words such as "*vache*" and "*glace*" and "*les choses, vous savez, pour les pieds comme ça,*" pointing to his big feet. Aina, still convinced that the Frenchman intended to cheat her of her cow, underscored these communications with a selection of dire and threatening gestures.

"Ring the dinner bell, Louise!" Lanthier told his wife, though it was just half past nine in the morning. "I have nine children, and I want them all to see a cow wearing boots," he explained to Uwe. Then he threw his head back and laughed aloud.

When all of the Lanthiers' nine children had assembled expectantly on the bank of the river, Old Farmer Lanthier threw a threadbare Hudson's Bay blanket over Olga's back, tied a rope about her neck and led her to Aina. "*Voilà, madame,*" he said. "*Votre vache!*"

Aina took the rope he offered her, handed it to Uwe and sat down on the ground next to the cow.

"Your boots," she instructed Uwe.

Reluctantly, with a sideways glance at the unruly crowd of Lanthiers, Uwe fished his extra pair of hobnailed boots out of his packsack and handed them to Aina. She pulled them on over her rubber moccasins, lacing them up tightly. The boots were much too large for her, but the distance she had to go in them was short. What was important was that they gripped the ice.

"Olga will never consent to wear boots," Uwe hissed at Aina. "You bring disgrace on me, yourself, Finland!"

Aina thrust out her hand. "Olga's boots!" she ordered. "One at a time."

Uwe rummaged around in the packsack and brought

forth a boot. Aina, having been uncertain about left and right, front and back, as regards a cow's hoof, had made them all the same — a leather cup into the bottom of which a square of wood had been fitted to serve as a kind of sole. Two-inch spikes had been driven down through this sole so that they protruded out the other side. Around two of the spikes, placed on the left and right side of the sole, rawhide thongs had been tied. Aina intended to lash the boot to the cow's leg by means of these thongs. Lifting Olga's first leg, she carefully fitted the leather cup onto the heifer's hoof. Olga tried to kick, but Aina held her leg firmly.

"Now, you hold this leg," she shouted in Finnish to the biggest Lanthier boy. "*Vite! Vite!*" After repeating the command several times and pointing, she managed to convey to the boy her intention. He ran over and, dropping to his knees, seized Olga's leg and held it firmly while Aina tied the boot to it. Indicating to the boy to continue holding on to the heifer's leg, she then moved to the heifer's left front foot and fitted the next boot, pointing first to another one of Lanthier's children, a girl of about eight who was hunkered down to watch the show. "*Vite!*" she cried. "You there! *Vite!*" The girl sprang to her feet at once and bounded over to Olga. Dropping to her knees, she seized Olga's left front leg.

In this fashion and with the assistance of Lanthier's children, Aina managed to fit Olga with the homemade boots in about a quarter of an hour, despite the bewildered cow's plaintive protests. Alarmed at finding herself two inches taller than she was accustomed to being and perched precariously on twenty spikes, the heifer rolled her big, soft eyes and bawled plaintively, pitching her weight backwards, forwards and sideways in a desperate attempt to free herself of the four pairs of hands restraining her.

"Tell them, 'At the count of three, let go,'" Aina instructed Uwe, who, after several false starts, managed to convey this strategy to the children holding down the cow. Then Aina stood, and grasping the rope around Olga's neck, she ventured out onto the ice as far as the rope extended — about four feet. The ice was smooth, mirror-bright and as white as an eyeball. She nodded to Uwe to indicate that she was ready.

"*Un, deux, trois!*" cried Uwe.

Aina ground the heels of her hobnailed boots into the glare ice, leaned back and pulled with all her might. The children released Olga's legs, falling back into the snow, and the cow came skittering desperately out onto the ice, her legs tangling and chips of green ice flying. But Aina did not pause. She knew that if she stopped, the cow would also stop, so she backed off across the river as fast as she could, sliding and skidding and dragging Olga along with her. Olga, meanwhile, convinced that she had miraculously escaped some dire fate when she had broken free of the children's grasp, tottered gingerly after Aina, her ears flapping, her tail flicking and her spiked boots making a rat-a-tat sound like hail hitting a roof.

In a moment's time, they were on the other side of the river (it was, after all, not a very big river), and Olga, staggering desperately from right to left, kicked first one leg, then the other in an attempt to free herself of the spiked boots.

On the opposite bank, the Lanthiers and Uwe cheered and clapped and jumped up and down. "Bravo!" cried the children.

"There, there," Aina advised the cow. Kneeling beside her, she caught at her front leg and began to untie the rawhide thong. "You're all right now, my Olga. You will never have to wear boots again."

Uwe jogged across the ice to join Aina.

"How smart you are, Aina!" Uwe congratulated his wife. "How did you know that the cow would wear boots?"

"I didn't," said Aina shortly, not looking up at him but unlashing a second boot. "But I wanted my cow."

On the other side of the river, Lanthier turned to his wife. "Too bad about that heifer. I was going to sell her to Old Mercer next week. He took a fancy to her the last time he was here, and the Finn does not know enough to get a bill of sale when he buys livestock. Still, it was worth the money to see such a marvellous sight as a cow in boots."

Uwe was right about one thing: Olga was a companion to Aina, and once the cow came to the farm, Aina, who had been so glum and sour the whole winter long, seemed to Uwe almost happy. What he didn't know was that his little wife soothed herself to sleep at night thinking up ingenious ways to murder him using ordinary household objects or such implements as one might find about a farm — the scythe he used for cutting the tall grass, for example, or the pitchfork with which he baled hay, or that coil of brass wire for snaring rabbits, or just that least little bit of lye poured into his whisky jug. Once he almost obliged her when a bottle of assayer's acid in the back pocket of his trousers burst into flames over at the blind pig in Cobalt, but a drunk prospector rolled the big Finn up in a blanket and put out the fire. It was a long time before Uwe could sit comfortably on his left buttock, however, and that gave Aina some satisfaction.

As for Uwe, he watched his young wife sing her way busily through her day, seemingly happy at her tasks and content, and he thought that he had been right to marry her, after all, and wasn't it about time to go into town for nails or tarpaper or, better yet, for seed? Sooner or later, he was going to need seed if he was going to farm this land. And he'd take up his snowshoes and say to Aina, "I'll be back tomorrow or maybe the next day."

"Yes, yes, go along, then," she would say, hoping that he might be eaten by a bear or attacked by wolves or catch his leg in a trap and freeze to death. One thing was for sure: a man could die a hundred ways in this wilderness.

At the first touch of the vernal sun, in late May of that year, the entire countryside around the farm grew loose and wobbly in its joints, like an overcooked fowl. The snow sunk and shrank with loud sighs. Bare patches of soggy ground spread like brown stains on the previously white face of the land. A brook pulsed through every ravine; a river twisted through every valley. On the river, water stretched in shining pools a foot deep across the ice, while the muskegs thereabouts grew bottomless and quaked, as if with some deep hunger. The half-cleared field out back became a lake, the stumps that littered it submerged by a good foot and a half of water.

By this time, Aina was pregnant. She would not have known of her condition had not Madame Lanthier looked twice at her that time she came buying eggs and said as much. After consulting with several neighbour ladies, whom she had convened for the express purpose of determining how far along Aina was through pantomime, discussion and examination, Madame Lanthier concluded that the girl was due sometime in October. These particulars was conveyed with some difficulty to Aina, who still spoke no English or French.

Aina's feelings about her condition were mixed. On the one hand, she was pleased that she would soon have additional companionship in the form of a child; on the other hand, having a baby in tow would make escape from Uwe more difficult.

As for Uwe, the revelation at once delighted and panicked him. "A son!" he exalted. "The Pahakka line will live on in our child!" On occasions when his mood was less sanguine, however, he despaired. "Another mouth to feed! And I have a hard enough time feeding a woman and a cow!"

"The cow feeds herself," Aina pointed out. "And I feed you."

After a week of trying to clear the field using a big dray horse he had rented by the day from Old Farmer Lanthier, Uwe gave up. "This land is useless, and what am I going to grow anyway?" he asked Aina. "Potatoes like Old Farmer Lanthier? Turnips? The growing season is too short and the soil is too full of rocks. No, I am going up to Golden City and see if I can get work at that Hollinger mine there. I hear they're hiring every able-bodied man who walks through the dry-room door. Maybe I'll do some prospecting first. That's the way to get rich: find gold. Drill, blast, scale and timber . . . Farming is for fools. Later, I'll send for you."

Mining accidents were not infrequent, Aina mused. There were gas leaks, and she had heard of hoist cables breaking, hurtling miners to their deaths, and rock exploding when a miner bit his drill into the side of a drift and hit a missing hole. As for prospectors, they tended to just wander off.

"Buy me a pig and some chickens, and I'll put in vegetables where you've cleared," she told Uwe. "Then you can go to the Porcupine and we will have eggs and bacon and ham, too, once the winter comes. The baby is not due until the fall. Olga and I will be fine."

So Uwe bought a fat piglet from Old Farmer Lanthier and a rooster and two speckled hens, and in mid-June of 1911, he packed his packsack and caught the railway spur north to Golden City.

It started as a ground fire, burning perhaps for weeks in the moss and humus that made up the forest floor around the tarpaper shack. The air smelled acrid, as if lightning had just struck a nearby tree. Aina's eyes smarted for days.

"The summer is hot, too hot," Madame Lanthier observed, sniffing the air and blinking. "It's a summer for fire, all right."

In July, a surface fire boiled up from the humus, a lick of flame that caught and held the attention of the bush. It spread, eating the deadfalls and windrows over a two- to three-hectare radius to the west of Aina and Uwe's farm.

"You can contain a brush fire," Old Farmer Lanthier reassured her. "It's the crown fires you have to watch out for. Thank the Blessed Virgin there's no wind."

Of course, all Aina understood was the word "fire" and the fact that Old Farmer Lanthier didn't seem to be too alarmed. The Lanthiers did want Aina to stay with them, however. "We insist," they said. "Just till the fire is contained."

But Aina shook her head. "I have left my Olga at home," she told them, "and the pig and the chickens. I must go back."

The Lanthiers, of course, understood only that she had refused their offer. "Stupid woman," exclaimed Old Farmer Lanthier, watching Aina pole across the river on the raft he had spiked together that spring out of dry jack pines.

For the following three days, men from the township fought the surface fire, hauling buckets of water from the river and digging trenches. Then, on the third night, the wind picked up and blew flames upwards, into the tall tops of the trees. The gas and chemicals in the burning leaves exploded, generating strong winds that, in turn, drove the fire before them; flames leapt from tree to tree like frenzied dancers. At the same time, the surface fire abated; the new crown fire had sucked the air beneath the treetops up into itself to feed on, creating a kind of vacuum along the ground.

Unlike the brush fire, which had gone about its destruction in a slow, methodical fashion, cropping the undergrowth as sheep or cattle will systematically graze a field, the crown fire was chaotic and greedy. By midnight, the corduroy road leading to Aina's house was lined by blazing fires that roared like a dozen freight trains converging on the same crossing at once. She could hear nothing over the fire's high, insistent shriek, and the heat from the blaze scorched her skin as red as the noonday sun might. The night was as bright as day, fire-lit and teeming with shadows.

Aina doused the tarpaper shack with well water in the hopes that this might keep it from catching fire; then she poured a bucket of water over her own head to keep stray sparks from igniting her hair and clothing. Hastily, she assembled a bundle — her good dress, an extra pair of shoes, some tiny garments that she had sewn for the baby, a gold locket that had belonged to her maternal grandmother and some crumpled banknotes — rolled it up in a blanket and buried it a shallow hole she scraped out with her hands in the dirt floor in the root house. She figured that as the floor of the root house was three feet below ground level, it might withstand fire better than the shack.

Leaving the root house, she let the pig out of its sty and the chickens out of their coop. The pig promptly began to bury himself in the cool, moist manure pile next to the stick barn. The hens and the rooster, after a few moments of confused rushing back and forth and clucking and flapping, did the same, though less systematically.

Finally, Aina doused another blanket with water and, holding it over her head, ran through the boiling smoke towards the half-cleared field where she had put Olga out to pasture a few hours before. "I am coming, Olga!" she called to the heifer, but the fire's roar was so loud that she could not hear herself cry out; her words were swallowed up in the horrible howl.

Just as she reached the field, she stumbled over a root and pitched forward onto her hands and knees in the sticky mud of the half-ploughed earth. To the west, the fire snapped and licked its way along the stump fence that separated the clearing from the forest. A hot pine cone exploded; its flying fragments drove into her cheek. She cried out; the fragments stung like shrapnel.

Then, as she was struggling to rise, an undulating serpent of flame coiled through the fire-lit sky high above her, idle as a kite that drifts and hangs upon the air before suddenly it plunges. Aina rose to her knees in the mud, transfixed by the sight of the serpentine flame, unable to move as it spiralled down towards her, frightened but not knowing how to avoid it, which way to twist or turn so that it would not fall on her. In fact, it slid past her shoulder by little more than a hand's breadth, and died, writhing like some damned and tormented soul, in the muck beside her.

Aina gasped with relief, then blinked. Everything had gone dark, indistinguishable. She blinked again, but still she could not separate images from the dull blackness that lay against her eyes. Unlike darkness, this blackness had no depth; it was flat and crowded close against her. She closed her eyes and felt them burn against the membrane that lined her eyelid. The flame's heat must have seared her corneas. She had heard of that happening — temporary blindness that might take hours to heal, or weeks. At any rate, for now Aina could not see.

"Olga! Olga!" she cried, reaching out with both hands to feel the space around her. Her fingers closed shut on air. "Olga! Are you there?" she shrieked into the gale.

The fire screamed back its wordless fury, a maddened monster that cannot be appeased but must howl and howl and destroy everything within its grasp.

Pushing herself up with one hand, Aina stood with difficulty, wobbling for a moment when she had found her feet. Six months gone with child, her body had grown ungainly; it was more difficult for her to find her balance than before, particularly now, when she could not see. Tentatively, the Finnish woman stepped forward into the roaring nothingness before stumbling over another gnarled root. Cursing Uwe for not clearing the field, she ventured gingerly first this way, then that, feeling her way with her hands. But there were roots and charred stumps everywhere she turned. The dried branches tore at her scorched skin. They seemed to surround her.

After a few moments of trying to find her way through the field of stumps, Aina gave up. She did not know which direction she was facing, where she had been, where she might hope to find the cow. "Olga!" she cried again, but without hope now of any reply. Weary and distraught, she sunk down onto one knee, then both. Then she sat with her legs stretched out before her. Finally, she dropped down onto her side in the cool muck of the open, haphazardly ploughed field, pulled her knees up towards her belly, and drew the wet blanket over her head, shoulders and torso. Miraculously, she slept.

Aina opened her eyes just a crack. They were very sore, but by squinting and shading them with her hand, she could just make out the outline of the sun, newly risen in the east. Glimpsed through the thick boil of settling smoke, it looked more like the moon than itself — a pale, anemic disc, more reflective than radiant. I am not blind after all, she marvelled.

Stiff and sore and still shading her eyes with her hands, for the light made them ache, Aina stood carefully and peered around the field. The soil was as dry as snuff under her feet and reflected heat like an oven. She took a step forward. At her footfall, ashes whirled up, clogging her nostrils. She sneezed, then coughed, then realized that the sound she heard inside of her head was her ears ringing. Was the fire over, then? She could no longer hear its roar, nor could she see flames, just smoke and ash and the burnt black shape of things. . . .

Suddenly, Aina stopped and stared straight ahead.

A black cow stood forlornly in the far northwest corner of the field.

Aina took a tentative stop towards her.

Who could this black cow be? she wondered. Not Olga. Olga was a brindled cow — red and grey and brown. Where had this black cow come from?

Aina took another step.

Was she one of Old Farmer Lanthier's cows? How had she crossed the river? Perhaps she belonged to someone else. There were new neighbours to the south . . .

Then it struck her. She stopped in her tracks, absorbing the blow by doubling over it and twisting to one side — it was as though she had been punched in the stomach, hard. "Olga?" she exhaled.

Slowly, the cow turned its big head to look at her.

Afraid but unable to stop herself, Aina stumbled head-long towards the heifer. "Olga," she pleaded.

The cow lowed.

Aina crept up alongside the burnt heifer. She looked first at one side of her, then the other. Then, assembling the fragments of her remaining courage, she reached out with shaking fingers to touch Olga's blackened coat. As she had feared, her fingers came in contact not with Olga's sweet silky hide but with a crisp, thick crust. Where Aina's fingers had touched the animal, the crust peeled off in a great welt, leaving a flaming red patch, raw and bare.

"Oh, Olga!" Aina exclaimed.

Moving to the front of the heifer, she stared hard into the animal's eyes. They were flat and opaque like stones, river rocks, not soft and jelly-like as they had been before. Olga had not been so lucky as Aina. The fire had burnt away her retinas. She was blind.

Aina dropped to her knees and, looking underneath the cow, cried aloud, then bit her hand in anguish. Olga's hooves and udders were utterly gone, burnt away. "I don't understand," Aina whispered hoarsely to the heifer. "How can you even be alive?"

But Olga only lowered her head and blindly tried to browse the blackened grass with fumbling lips.

Aina rose to her feet, shaking so violently that she was not certain that her body could contain her. Weeping, she staggered towards the root house, where Uwe kept a loaded shotgun — for wolves or bears or other fierce creatures that might threaten the farm.

Later that morning, Uwe returned. He had heard about the fire up in Golden City, and had commandeered a handcart and ridden the rails south to Cobalt to see if Aina needed any help.

"It's too bad you weren't able to save the house," he told her. She was crouched in the yard by the root house, watching disconsolately as the pig dug its way out of the manure pile. The rooster and one hen staggered around the yard, covered with dung. The other hen had died, somehow burnt alive suffocated by smoke or manure.

"Did you tell anyone where you were going?" Aina wanted to know. Her voice was flat. She seemed worn out to Uwe. She didn't once look at him or seem excited to see him. To tell the truth, the Finn was not a little put out. He hadn't caused the fire, after all, and he had come as soon as he had heard.

"Not likely," Uwe reassured her. "The T&NO doesn't take kindly to a fellow borrowing its handcart."

"Good." Aina seemed satisfied.

Later, when Uwe's back was turned, Aina shot him. She used the same shotgun with which she had dispatched Olga — there were two shells in it, after all. She buried both her husband and the cow in a big hole in the field. It took her the better part of a day to dig the hole and another to fill it, but when it was done, she felt much better, though she still missed Olga.

The next day, she dug up the bundle of clothing she had buried in the root house. The locket was blackened and the banknotes singed; still, there was enough money to tide her over until she could sell the farm.

In early October 1911, just a few days shy of her first wedding anniversary and after thirty-six hours of a difficult labour, Aina Pahakka gave birth to a plump, ice-eyed daughter whom she named Olga. Madame Lanthier brought the baby into the world, having had much experience in these matters.

Regrettably, Olga's father, Uwe Pahakka, had gone missing some months earlier. He had last been seen in the area of Golden City about the time of the Great Fire in Cobalt. Perhaps he had gone prospecting and lost his way in the bush. These things had been known to happen, and Uwe had always been a careless, easy sort of man, prone to mishaps and mistakes.

Or perhaps he had grown tired of married life and gone West.

The following spring, when he still hadn't turned up, Aina sold the farm to a settler from Southwestern Ontario and booked passage back to Finland with her young daughter.

"You can't say I didn't warn you," her father told her upon her arrival home. "I always knew that Uwe Pahakka was no good!"

Aina did not marry the farmer's sturdy, tow-headed son, about whom she had dreamed for so many months, for he was married already to her sister, Olga. However, in time, she married another farmer's son, to whom she quickly bore five children and with whom she came to own and maintain one of the very best dairy farms in their little region, with several strong bulls and many fine brindled heifers.

THE PROSPECTOR'S BOOT

When her mother and younger sister died suddenly of black diphtheria in the summer of 1909, Emma Trudgian wired the news to her father in Cobalt. Two weeks later, having given some thought to her future, she sent a second wire, informing her father (who had not, as yet, replied to her first telegram) that she was coming north to keep house for him. Then, without waiting for a reply (since it was by no means certain that a wire sent to Cobalt would reach her father in the mining camp of South Porcupine in any case), she bought a one-way ticket on the Temiskaming and Northern Ontario Railway to Kelso. The railway went only as far as Kelso.

By Emma's reckoning, heading north was her only real option. She was unmarried and, at twenty-one, too old for a Home. Her father, though a stranger to her, was now her only living relation in Canada. The rest of the Trudgians and the Arthurs (her mother's family) lived in a little hamlet called Brannel near St. Austell in Cornwall and had to do with clay pits, the spinning of wool and turbary.

Of course, in the week following the death of Emma's mother and sister, the Reverend Mr. Evans, her mother's spiritual adviser and former euchre partner, had managed to dredge up a suitable beau for a severe girl of no fortune after some fishing and poking about the stagnant waters of his flock — Mr. McLachlan, a tall, stooped Scotsman, newly arrived in Canada. Mr. McLachlan was thirty-eight years old, had green, tangled teeth and smelled like bundled-up, damp wool.

Emma, however, had demurred. "My father needs me to keep house," she had told the clergyman.

"What house?" Mr. Evans had wondered.

"Well . . . cabin," Emma had clarified.

Mr. McLachlan, Mr. Evans had assured her, would most certainly be crestfallen. However, the minister had other bereaved to comfort. Before he could call on her again, Emma had left for the North.

Emma's father was named Edward Trudgian. He was a prospector. Once, he had been a bank clerk. He had worn a white paper collar around his neck and a visor and had written entries in a copperplate hand in big ledgers at the Bank of Commerce downtown. The talk around the bank at the time was all of the Klondike and the Yukon, where gold had recently been discovered. Gold is, after all, of great interest to persons in and about banks. Customers told tales of rough men who had lived all their lives in the bush, pushing wheelbarrows filled with placer gold panned from the rushing northern rivers about the tent cities that littered the Klondike, as though what they so casually transported were rocks or dirt or sod. Their pockets bulged with nuggets the size of quail eggs that they picked directly off the ground.

Edward bent closer over his ledgers when he heard such stories; he wished to appear to be concentrating on his work. Then, one day, he told his manager that he must go home to Cornwall to see his dying mother (she had, in fact, died years before). Instead, he bought a train ticket to Kingston, where he took a short course in geology at Queen's College. Then, bound for the Klondike, he boarded a ship headed round the Horn, telling Emma's distraught mother that he would soon be back. "I will be gone only long enough to make a fortune," he assured her. "Then I will return."

That was eight years ago. By the time he had reached the Yukon, six months later, it was all staked out, and so he had moved on to Alaska, where he prospected the Kayukuk at Cleary Creek.

Every four months or so, his wife received a letter, written in his impeccable, small hand. These letters she would read aloud to Emma and her sister. The letters were oddly formal and dwelt largely upon the character of the landscape, the geology and the weather.

My dear wife and daughters,

I have located a promising gabbro hill in my traipses — that is a hill made up of granular, igneous rock consisting principally of calcic plagioclase. . . . I dare not give the coordinates, lest this letter be intercepted and another jump my claim.

As for the rest, we are in a deep freeze here and have been since late December. It is hard to sleep. The ice on the lake booms continuously. . . .

He always concluded his letters in the same way:

I know in my heart that it will not be long before we are reunited as a family. Until then . . .

Later, as the months and then the years passed and still Edward did not return, her mother found that she lacked breath to read the letters aloud. Instead, she read them to herself, silently, before tucking them in a pocket of her apron or the bosom of her shirtwaist. Only after she had carried them about with her for some time would she pass them on to her daughters, as if reluctantly, for their perusal.

When Edward finally returned from Alaska, four years after his initial departure, he gave them no advance warning. Instead, he simply arrived on the doorstep of their Bedford Street home, carrying a bundle wrapped in yellowed American newspapers and tied tightly with string. When unwrapped, this bundle proved to be a tall stack of new, crisp five- and ten-dollar bills. He had staked more than thirty claims at Cleary Creek and done well on some of them.

It seemed to the women that he looked smaller than when he had first left them, hunched and little, with a grizzle of whiskers and hands dyed brown by the earth, clutching and unclutching. There was a smell about him too, no matter how much he scrubbed — sickly sweet and reminiscent of carrion. This was fly dope, which over time had settled deep into his pores.

Edward remained in Toronto for one week and five days. Years in the bush had made him restless; he could not sit still, and the street traffic outside the window made him jump. At night, by their mother's side, he could not sleep. Although neither Emma nor her sister would have admitted it, they were relieved when he headed north to check out the new silver claims at Mile 103 of the T&NO Railway. "I won't be gone long," he promised their mother. "This time I will make my fortune, and then we can all be together again."

After his departure, Mrs. Trudgian took to her bed for a week.

In the year leading up to Emma's mother's and sister's deaths, the Trudgians had heard from Edward three times, once from Boston Creek, once from Kirkland Lake, and the last time, just four months earlier, from South Porcupine.

"The quartz here is very promising," he had written. "It runs in thick veins under the muskeg, a milky white, and its texture is like sugar. I have built a little cabin, with a backhouse." He ended this letter, as he did all the others, in the usual way: "I know in my heart that it will not be long before we are reunited as a family. Until then . . ."

The train trip to Kelso took seventeen hours. At first, the land outside the window seemed familiar, but after a while the earth's big bones came poking through its green skin — shoulder blades and ribs and rough knees of granite, pink in the sun. The vegetation also altered, the hardwood forests yielding to jack pine, spruce and tamarack. The land to either side of the tracks was pocked with lakes mirroring the blue sky. The land became bigger, the sky smaller, and the air turned chill.

The train was full of men, some Indians. Many of the men spoke a rasping French that scraped away at Emma's ear like a bow dragged rustily across the strings of a man-handled fiddle. Others spoke a rough English, burred and ragged with oaths. They drank from gallon jugs of Catawba red wine that they passed between them, wiping the top of the bottle each time with the tails of their red flannel shirts. Spread-legged, they played noisy cards on big, dusty knees.

"*Vite! Vite! Vite!*" they insisted. "*Alors!*"

"Mary, mother o' God, an' where'd dat be comin' from? I warn you, O'Connor: you're a dead man."

The Indians laughed gently and pointed at one another and sometimes out the window. They spoke a tongue she had not heard before. It sounded like eels slipping loosely together.

The man who sat down next to her, however, was not French or Indian, or rough, but a polite, small Englishman named Mr. Watkins. He was going to South Porcupine to establish a branch of the Bank of Montreal.

"I am going to South Porcupine as well," she told him. "To keep house for my father."

Mr. Watkins looked at her with surprise. "From what I

hear, South Porcupine's little more than bush," he advised her. For a young man, he was quite bald and his eyebrows were so pale as to be invisible, giving his face a clean, wiped look.

"My father has a log cabin," she assured him.

"Moose!" shouted someone at the front of the car. A half a dozen men leapt to their feet. Cards flew. The jug of wine, dropped, rolled lopsidedly down the aisle, leaving a trail like thin, scarlet blood down the soiled carpet. Three men noisily cranked down stiff windows while others rummaged, cursing and shouting, under seats and in overhead compartments for rifles and pistols. Seconds later, four shots rang out and there was an acrid smell in the air of spent powder and smoke. Men laughed and congratulated one another. Someone asked, "Did we get him?"

When Emma got off the train at Kelso, her father was not there. There was, however, a hostel buried in the bush about five hundred feet from the tracks. At first, fleetingly, she mistook it for a stand of young birch — it was dusk by then — but after a moment, she made it out well enough: a long, low building fashioned from peeled logs chinked with dried moss. Its foundation was banked high with earth, to keep the logs from rotting with the frost, and black tarpaper, curling and cracking at the edges from exposure to the elements, was loosely tacked over a roof that appeared to be made of poles lashed together. She could smell the woodsmoke, which coiled lazily out of an unstable-looking stone chimney piled haphazardly against one wall of the hostel, and turpentine and pitch as well. Blackflies and mosquitoes swarmed about her, probing interestedly at her exposed flesh, biting and stencilling.

"What? What?" cried Mr. Watkins, surprised at this onslaught, swatting.

A French trader named Hermidos Germain owned the hostel. He told Emma that there were no messages from her father.

"Is it possible that he could not have received my wires?" she wondered.

The trader shrugged. "How am I to know?" Germain's leathery skin was the flat colour of a walnut, his eyes were yellow like a cat's and he wore his long grey hair tied back with a length of rawhide. "One thing for sure: a wire from Cobalt does not fly to South Porcupine. It might walk, but only if it has a man with two legs to carry it."

He was clearly put out at Emma's arrival. "What are you doing here?" he asked. "No women come here. We have one room only, all bunk beds for men. Well, you will have to sleep with my wife, which means that I cannot. As for you . . ." He turned to Watkins. "You sleep with the men. Tomorrow we will find somebody to take the two of you into the Porcupine. Or maybe the next day."

"I have a brother," Angele clarified. Angele was the trader's wife, an Ojibwa woman. "My brother is not here now," explained Angele, "but he may be back soon." She was a sturdy woman, fat and plain, like bannock. From the darkness of her hair and the smoothness of her skin, Emma judged her to be her own age, possibly younger. Angele wore a beaver coat that hung open to reveal a kind of shift fashioned from a split flour sack. The shift was decorated with beads. It seemed to Emma that Angele might be pregnant, though it was difficult to tell because of the looseness of the shift.

Later, when they were getting ready for bed, Angele handed Emma a battered tin canister with a perforated lid.

"What is this for?" Emma asked.

Angele gestured to the straw ticking on which Emma was to sleep. "*La! La!*" she encouraged her. "It's bug powder."

Later, when she had turned down the feed on the coal-oil lamp and blown out the flame, she told Emma, "My name is not really Angele. That is just what he calls me."

Three days later, Angele's brother returned to the hostel. In the summer he was a guide. In the winter he trapped furs and sold them to Revillon Frères or the Hudson's Bay Company, whichever post he happened to be closest to. His name was Billy Big Blood, and he agreed to take Emma and Mr. Watkins to South Porcupine for $3.50 each.

Taking a boy with them to help with the portaging, they left Kelso at seven in the morning for Frederick House Lake, canoed across it and up the Frederick House River to Hill's Landing, then they portaged the canoe to Three Nations Lake, canoed across it, and portaged to Bob's Lake and into South Porcupine.

On the way, Mr. Watkins attempted to engage the guide in conversation. "How do the Indians tell how severe the coming winter will be?" he wanted to know. "I've read that they observe the thickness of animals' fur or how much food squirrels collect or how many rosehips there are on a rose. . . ."

"Those are good ways," conceded Billy Big Blood. Like his sister he was heavily built, but he was also very tall. His face was pitted from smallpox. "But let me tell you the best way. The Indian watches the white man. He watches him very carefully. And when he sees the white man chopping much wood, then he knows it will be a very cold winter."

They arrived just after supper at the untidy profusion of shacks, stumps and tents, mired in mud, that was the mining camp of South Porcupine. Mr. Watkins took it upon himself to ask around for Edward Trudgian — given that Emma was a young woman travelling alone, he, as a gentleman and representative of the Bank of Montreal, felt responsible for the plain, awkward girl and wished to discharge his duties towards her as quickly as possible.

After a few failed attempts, he came upon a group of men hunkered around a campfire, cooking up a bush rabbit with some beans in a tin can. "Eddie Trudgian! Sure I know him," said a grizzled old prospector in a black, knitted woollen cap and a soiled, fringed buckskin coat. "Went around the Horn with him years ago. Don't live hereabouts no more. Up towards Gilies Lake. That's where he is. Got that whole hill up there staked out. Big knob of white quartz. You can't miss it. See it sticking up above the trees. Due west of here. Not far."

"I might take you there tomorrow," speculated Billy Big Blood. He had been following Mr. Watkins around on his investigations. "For a dollar."

That night Emma spent in Mr. Watkins's new white tent. The bank manager slept on the ground with Billy Big Blood, his face swathed in cheesecloth, his body wrapped in the rabbitskin robe of some unfortunate who had wandered off into the bush two weeks before, never to return. The blackflies and the mosquitoes rattling against the canvas of Mr. Watkins's tent sounded to Emma like a driving rain that did not cease all night; they made a low humming sound like an organ.

The next morning, just as dawn was breaking over the camp, Emma, Mr. Watkins and Billy Big Blood headed west for Gilies Lake, following the old prospector's instructions. They could still see the moon when they started out — a gibbous crescent glimmering through veils of woodsmoke that hovered about fifteen feet above the ground. As there was nothing resembling even a bush trail to Gilies Lake, they were compelled to clamber over windfalls, strewn about the forest floor in disorderly heaps, to cover the scant five miles; windrows between the upturned roots of white birch and aspen struggled upwards to form dense thickets. Their faces and hands were already swollen and stinging with insect bites; now branches tore at their exposed flesh.

By eight in the morning, they had reached Pearl Lake, which lay just east of Gilies Lake. By nine, they had arrived on the shores of Gilies Lake itself. It was a very little lake, longer than it was wide, calm and mirror-bright under the cloudless sky. To the west, above the jagged treeline of spruces and tamaracks, rose the great knob of white quartz mentioned by the old prospector. A gauzy mist, left over from the night, swirled slowly around the reeds that grew near the shore. Red-winged blackbirds balanced lightly on swaying bulrushes.

It was very quiet.

They walked along the lake's southern shore, cutting up into the bush where the prospector had told them they could, on the west side, where there was faint evidence of a trail. About two hundred feet into the bush and up the hill from the lake, they came upon Edward Trudgian's cabin in a stand of tall spruce.

The cabin measured a rough twenty by twenty-four feet. Like the hostel in Kelso, it was constructed of peeled logs chinked with moss and mudded with clay, and its pole roof was weatherproofed with curling tarpaper. On the porch, a pile of freshly cut jack pine and another, smaller one of green poplar stood seasoning, while out back, about twelve feet from the cabin, a backhouse, built on the slope, leaned against a large boulder planted farther down the incline. The cabin's two windows, covered with smoke-stained oilcloth, were dark.

"Anyone home?" called Mr. Watkins.

"Papa?" called Emma.

No one answered.

"He may have gone out," suggested Mr. Watkins. "He may be prospecting."

They entered the cabin, leaving the door open for light.

The interior walls were whitewashed with lime. On the floor there was a kind of mattress or ticking, woven of balsam boughs, over which a tarpaulin and then a Hudson's Bay blanket had been thrown. Under one of the windows stood a table made from a packing crate and covered with a piece of oilcloth. A coal-oil lamp and some papers, some loose, others stacked and tied with string, and a half-dozen dog-eared notebooks were on the table. Under the other window there was a kind of chair fashioned from an empty biscuit barrel stuffed with a flour sack. In the corner opposite the bed stood an oval tin stove connected to a stove-pipe that ran through a roof jack to the outside.

A number of objects were scattered about on the mattress.

"Look," said Billy Big Blood, crossing to the makeshift bed. He knelt beside it. "A pick, his axe, a compass . . . This is what he had in his packsack." Turning around to look over his shoulder, he spotted something else — the packsack itself, lying crumpled in the corner behind the stove. Standing, he crossed to the stove and picked up the half-empty packsack. "Your father was looking for something in his packsack," he told Emma. "He found it, then left. He has not gone far. He would not have gone into the bush without these things."

They made themselves tea in Edward Trudgian's tea pail and waited. When the sun was climbing towards noon, they grew impatient and set out to look for the prospector. Just after one o'clock, on the other side of the quartz knob, about a quarter of a mile from Edward Trudgian's cabin, they found a crater in the ground. The crater was about six feet wide and a foot and a half deep. The vegetation around the crater was blasted and black; it was filled with wet ash and smelled like soggy gunpowder. In the trees around there were rags and tatters of bloody clothing and, low down, caught on the branch of a young spruce tree, one hobnailed boot.

Billy Big Blood showed Emma the boot. It was blackened and the hobnails were melted into irregular studs. She held the boot out to look at it. It was small, perhaps a size eight or nine. Her father had had small feet. Then she held the boot to her nose and smelled it. It smelled like gunpowder and char, but it also smelled like her father, a combination of the chilly inside of a marble bank and fly dope.

"It happened a few days ago," Billy Big Blood explained. "It has rained since then. He sat on a case of dynamite and lit the fuse. Or maybe he was drunk and dropped a lighted cigarette by mistake."

"Papa didn't drink," said Emma. "He never smoked."

Mr. Watkins urged Emma to come back to South Porcupine with him. Billy Big Blood said that he would take her back to the train for four dollars. However, Emma said that she would stay on for a while at Gilies Lake.

"How can you even think of staying?" Mr. Watkins demanded. "Out here in the bush by yourself! There are bears out here, timber wolves . . ."

"Indians," Billy Big Blood added.

"This isn't Toronto," concluded Mr. Watkins.

Emma glanced about her father's cabin. "There is Pa's rifle," she noted. "There's flour and tea and sugar and beans. He lived here well enough. I will be all right."

At last they consented to leave her for a fortnight, after which Mr. Watkins would send someone to check on her.

"There was nothing for it," Mr. Watkins defended his actions to those men back at South Porcupine who found his abandonment of Edward Trudgian's daughter in the bush difficult to comprehend. "You remember what a tall, big-boned woman she was? Well, I could hardly have been expected to pick her up and throw her over my shoulder and haul her back to South Porcupine, now could I have?" Mr. Watkins was such a diminutive man that the idea was ludicrous.

After Mr. Watkins and Billy Big Blood left, as dusk fell, Emma pulled the biscuit-tin chair in front of the little table, lit the coal-oil lamp and began to sort through the papers on the desk. Those bound with string turned out to be all the letters that her mother had written him over the eight years since his departure for the Yukon. There were forty-two of them. On top of the loose papers was the wire that she had sent him concerning her mother's and her sister's deaths, and beside it, a letter, never sent but addressed to her mother, her sister and her, dated just a few days before her wire. "I have found gold here by Gilies Lake," he wrote. "I cannot reveal the coordinates for the usual reasons, but I feel sure that I have discovered a remarkable vein not far from where I am writing. Free gold looking for all the world like globs of candle wax dripped onto the quartz." He ended this letter as he had all the others: "I feel sure that we shall be together shortly. Until then . . ."

Crumpling the unsent letter into a ball and hurling it into the corner by the stove, Emma leapt to her feet and cried out in a ragged voice, "If only you could have seen how they suffered, Papa! How they died! It was terrible to watch! Terrible! And you were nowhere, nowhere to be seen! You were never anywhere to be seen! You left and never came back, even though you said you would, and now you've gone and blown yourself up and left me all alone!"

She lunged about the cabin, kicking everything within reach of her foot until the floor was littered with balsam needles from the pillow and the mattress and with blue tin cups and battered granite chip plates and fishing tackle and twine and rolls of codline and pieces of yellow paper and cast-iron fry pans and awls and gimlets and knives for everything and boxes of steel traps and a half-dozen mouse-traps and tumbled flannelette sheets and long underwear, stiff with dirt, and grey woollen socks and toques and melton hats and deerskin mitts, all smelling like the boot, all smelling like him.

Then she went out on the porch, to breathe the cool night air in deep draughts. A solitary loon wailed its melancholy cry from the lake; the poignant wail exploded at the end in a burst of maniacal laughter. Emma re-entered the cabin and picked everything up, replacing it in what seemed its right place. Plumping up the battered mattress as best she could, she lay down to sleep under the Hudson's Bay blanket. The smell of balsam, sharp in her nose from the pillow and the mattress, almost drove the smell of her father from the threadbare blanket.

Emma did not leave with the man sent to check on her two weeks later — this same man conveyed with him the second telegram she had sent her father, the one announcing her arrival. It had just been delivered to South Porcupine by a prospector who had picked it up while registering a claim at Cobalt but then stopped for a piece on Night Hawk Lake before returning to the camp.

Nor did she leave with the men sent to check on her a month later and a month after that. Instead, she stayed, studying her father's copious notes on the claims he had staked, written in that fine copperplate hand in the notebooks he had left piled on the table. She laid aside the dresses and skirts and blouses she had brought with her from Toronto and took to wearing her father's old clothes. Like him, she took up his packsack and his pick and his axe and his compass and his mineral glass and roamed about the bush near the cabin, looking for gossan or burn, the stain on a rock that suggests the oxidization of metallic minerals, looking for the free gold that he had described in his last, unsent letter to his family — the gold that looked like candle wax dribbled on the rock.

In the autumn of that year, Emma noticed that one of the mallards whose flock had that summer colonized the shallows on the west end of the lake had injured its right wing. When she approached the lake to fish, the other ducks would rise up from the reeds and fly squawking away, leaving the injured duck to swim round and round in a tight circle by itself.

As the weather grew colder, the lake began to scum with ice. The mallard flock moved south. One morning when Emma arrived at the lake, they were gone, leaving only the injured duck behind.

As long as there was open water, the duck continued to fend well enough for itself. It could not fly, but it could fish and it could swim. However, as the ice thickened and extended to cover more of the lake, the circle of open water in which it swam grew smaller and smaller.

One day in late October, after a particularly cold night, Emma went down to the lake to see a circular area of sea green where the last stretch of open water had been — it was newly formed ice. Near the circle lay two feathers and three spots of crimson blood. Two sets of dainty fox prints, evenly spaced, like pearls on a string, led up to the circle of ice and then away from it. The mallard was nowhere to be seen.

As Emma turned to go, one of the duck's iridescent feathers, driven by the cold, sharp wind, tumbled end over end across the hard drifts before her and then, lifted by a second breeze, wafted upwards and whirled away to catch on the branch of a willow tree growing near the shore, and to stick.

PAPER SON

Ah Sing was not his real name. Ah Sing was the name of his paper father, the man from whom he had purchased the identity that would allow him to immigrate to Canada. The Benevolent Society, to which both his family and that of the real Ah Sing belonged, had negotiated the transaction. For Ah Sing, a native of Hoiping, was retiring from Canada to Sze Yap, and the new Immigration Act permitted only those Chinese with relatives living in the country before 1923 to enter.

"Ah Sing does not wish to die in the barbarians' land, leaving his bones to moulder seven years in a foreign house of the dead before they can be returned to the ancestral graveyard," his relations explained. "He prefers to bring his bones back himself."

Everyone agreed that, truly, it would be the worst kind of joss for Ah Sing to leave his bones in a strange land and forgo the veneration owed him by subsequent generations. To avoid such a misfortune, the Chinese in America and Canada and Australia had established dead houses in which they interred their departed for a period not to exceed seven years, after which the bones were scraped clean of what particles of flesh and portions of queues and matted hair still adhered to them and then were shipped back to their former owner's place of origin in ceramic pots.

Besides, his relatives proudly continued, Ah Sing was well able to afford the passage home . . . and more. For twenty years, he had travelled up and down Vancouver Island in an old wagon, selling vegetables and battered fruit from door to door, enduring the savage taunts of barbarian children and living no better than a dog or a pig but always saving his money in an old tea chest, until now he had at least seven hundred dollars. By Kwantung standards, Ah Sing could be counted a rich man, and he was ready to come home to sire a son and to die.

This was the false Ah Sing's ambition — to make his fortune in Canada and return to his village of Yanping in silken robes. Better that than trying to scratch out a living on his father's farm, where the soil was too leached out to grow anything but some rice and a stand of poppies for opium, and where there were always too many people needing to be fed. No, like an alien bent on plundering a distant planet, the false Ah Sing planned to descend upon the rough, barbarous place called Canada, take all he could and fly away.

His real name was Tai Soong, and he had turned nineteen the day he crept into the hold of the big steamship bound for British Columbia. It was just before dawn, bitingly cold, and the ship's hold stank of coal and rot and bilge and fish. To the fragile youth squatting in the recesses of the vessel so that the boiler men would be unable to distinguish him from its other cargo, it seemed like the cold, resonant belly of a whale.

It took the false Ah Sing three and a half years to work his way across Canada as far as Timmins, Ontario, a city not a decade old and the beating heart of the Porcupine country. He worked on the Canadian Pacific most of the way, riding boxcars east when he wasn't laying track or setting dynamite to blast rock.

It was hard work the Chinese did on the railway. MacAuliffe, the Scottish foreman, viewed them as just so much human flotsam: the Yellow Tide, he called them. They were so clearly of a grosser, inferior race — not only were they impervious to fatigue and hunger and pain ("It's because their nerve endings aren't as close to their skin as Europeans' are," MacAuliffe maintained. "Scientific fact."), but they also appeared to be completely insensible to personal danger. Because of this, and because there were so many of them competing for jobs on the railway, MacAuliffe saw the Chinese as an infinitely renewable resource and so assigned to them all the most perilous jobs. Accordingly, in the course of his employment by the CP, the paper son saw three of his fellow Chinese railway workers blown to bits, one dismembered, one buried alive through a miscalculation, one fall to a terrible death in a deep gorge, and two drowned in a raging river and then battered against big rocks until there was very little left of them to send back to the house of the dead in Vancouver. Fortunately for Ah Sing, he was a methodical youth, careful to a degree that irritated MacAuliffe and made him bluster and yell, "What the hell are you doing up there, Chinaman? Just light the damn thing and let's get on with this!" Still, the paper son survived, and that, he wrote his family back in Yanping, was something.

When he arrived in Timmins, however, he discovered to his great distress that there was no work for him in the mines. He went to work in a laundry on Third Street instead.

"This is how it happened," explained Du Quong. Du Quong was the owner of the laundry; he had bought it with money earned at the Hollinger mine before the Chinese were excluded. "Once the shafts were blasted into the veins and the struts and beams safely installed, once the narrow-gorge track lines were laid, well, then the whites took over and we Chinese . . . we were no longer welcome in the mines." Du Quong shrugged. He was probably not as old as Ah Sing's father, but he looked like a grandfather. His white clothes clung to his shrivelled body; his sweat-bathed face looked like an over-boiled polyp. It was the steam. Despite the fact that the thermometer hanging outside the door registered thirty below and the wind howled up and down the street like an enraged demon, the laundry was stiflingly hot, its big plate-glass window perpetually fogged. "Then the unions stepped in and made it final," Du Quong continued. "No more Chinese. It's the law. Still, Ah Sing, there are other ways to get rich."

The bell that hung over the door to the laundry tinkled. Ah Sing and Du Quong peered through the steam to see an Irish housemaid, red-faced and bundled up in a coat and muffler caked with snow, stagger through the door with a heaping basket of linens. "Mary, mother of God, but this heathenish weather!" she said.

"Wantee washee, Missy Moira?" Du Quong asked in his quacky English.

The false Ah Sing worked in Du Quong's laundry for three months. Then he worked for Ah Foo at the New Moon Restaurant on Mountjoy Street, busing dishes and washing up. In June, however, Du Quong informed the paper son that he had learned from Young-Wo-Song, who had heard it from Si Long the egg man, that Dr. Kirby was in need of a Chinese houseboy.

"Not a female! Nossir!" Dr. Kirby was adamant on this point. "What's our usual order, Si Long? Just let the maid go a week ago. Don't know these things."

"Two dozen white, Dr. Kirby, sir," Si Long replied. "Missy no like brown."

"Me neither! Give me a white egg any day!" Dr. Kirby exclaimed. "Much better for you!" He fumbled with change. "One bit . . . two bits . . . No, that last maid was one of those Irish girls fresh off the boat from Montreal. What she didn't steal, she broke before getting herself with child by one of those Cornish miners. Found half the family silver in that pawnshop your people run over on Third Street.

The Persuasive Profit, I think it's called. There you go, Si Long, three bits and a little something for your trouble, though I tell you, with the prices you're charging, those hens of yours should be laying golden eggs. Hah!" Dr. Kirby patted Si Long on the shoulder so heartily that the diminutive egg man, caught off balance, stumbled forward. The physician was a big, awkward man, with large hands, enormous feet and a springy red beard that he had the barber clip as precisely as topiary. He was given to bursts of excited and almost boyish bonhomie with his peers, but was clumsily avuncular in his dealings with inferiors, a category that included patients as well as servants.

Also too talkative, Si Long thought now, with mounting irritation. The egg man had other customers, after all, housewives who would take him to task for being late. But Dr. Kirby was not yet finished explaining his situation to the Chinaman.

"No, Si Long," he continued. "Moira may be safely married now, but I haven't a doubt in this world that it was the girl's goings-on that drove my poor wife to distraction (that and the weather, of course, not to mention the last stillbirth), for my beautiful Lily has suffered from nervous exhaustion all winter long. Weak as a kitten! Barely able to dress herself, much less see to the house, and damned if I've got time to help her, with my patient load. So . . ." He came round to his point. "You'll spread the word around among your people that I need a houseboy?"

"Oh, yes, Dr. Kirby." Si Long assured him. "Right away. Si Long get Dr. Kirby very good houseboy."

Excellent, Dr. Kirby reflected as he watched Si Long climb into his battered wagon and touch the reins to the

big dray horse that pulled it. Just what his wife needed —
a quiet, deferential celestial, as docile as a lamb. Besides, he
would not have to pay a Chinaman nearly so much as a
white girl, however lowly her origins.

The false Ah Sing applied for the job and got it. Dr.
Kirby paid him $1.75 a day and provided his room and
board on top of that. The houseboy was given a half-day off
on Saturdays, took his meals in the kitchen and slept on a
wooden cot in the pantry.

The paper son was thrilled with his good fortune. He
had never lived so comfortably before, and at $12.25 a
week, he calculated, it would be no time before he could
return home a wealthy man.

Lily Kirby lay on her divan in the pale, milky sunlight that
drifted in through the bedroom window, thinking about
how she might summon the energy to rise now that Edgar
had left on his infernal rounds.

A tall woman with dove grey eyes and a volume of
wheat-coloured hair, Lily appeared almost boneless as she
languished on her couch, her torpor the legacy of a season
of nervous prostration. Her pallor was that of the sickroom;
there was a hollowness to her eyes and a smell about her
too — of something stale and sweet and too long encased.
She looked, on the one hand, ghastly. Her family down in
Aylmer would have said so. However, there was also a compelling sense in which the physician's ailing wife had never
appeared more beautiful than now, when illness had robbed

her cheeks of colour and her eyes of brightness, when the long failure of appetite had refined a figure otherwise overly inclined to fleshiness.

"She looks," as Dr. Kirby had advised the bartender at the Empire Hotel, "like the queen of the dead."

Lily couldn't bear to be up and about when Edgar was home. He seized upon her every gesture, her every movement, however fluttering and faltering, to pronounce her better, a well woman, even cured. The implication, of course, was that he had cured her. "There! Don't I detect some tinge of colour in that wan cheek? You're getting better by the minute, Lily! Now if we could only put some fat on you. Butter, cream and eggs!" She stirred like a rankled cat. As if she could take more than a little weak tea and biscuit, some broth at best. It made her weary to think about it.

"Ah Sing!" she called in a weak voice. "Oh, Ah Sing!"

A moment later, she heard the sound of the houseboy's cloth shoes on the stairs. Ah Sing materialized on the threshold in his cotton-wadded tunic and black skullcap.

"Yes. Good. Come in, Ah Sing," Lily instructed the servant. "I have been thinking that I might get up today."

"Missy better?" The houseboy cocked his head. He reminded her of Mrs. Sherbrooke's budgerigar. Bright-eyed. Feather-boned.

"Better?" Lily echoed and sighed. "No, Ah Sing, not better. Just . . . restless. Help me up now. I want to walk in the garden."

"Yes, missy." Ah Sing took her elbow and supported her as she stood. He remained at her side, not relinquishing his hold on her elbow, for an additional moment. This was to allow time for the dizziness to pass.

Lily had been horrified when Edgar told her he had hired a Chinese houseboy to replace Moira Flannery. Coming from Southern Ontario as she did, she had never had much contact with celestials and knew little about them save that they were said to be the worst sort of heathens, with barbarous customs and prone to trafficking in white slavery and opium.

In fact, Lily, thought now as Ah Sing handed her a mother-of-pearl-headed cane and, still supporting her by the elbow, assisted her towards the door, celestials made perfect servants. On that score, she must give Edgar his due. Ah Sing was nothing like Moira, with her insolent tongue and her lying ways.

And the fact that he was a man . . . Well, that had distressed her at first. After all, she was not a well woman, and so had to be expected to persist in some state of déshabillé. Yet the servant had never registered any surprise that Lily should be so often in her nightdress, or that her wrap should be unbuttoned, or that her hair should be in such perpetual disarray. Reaching up with one trembling hand, she patted the amber curls into some vague semblance of place before handing Ah Sing the cane and gripping the banister with both hands in preparation to descend the narrow flight of stairs.

Oh, but the act of walking downstairs was so difficult for her now! The effort made her perspire and her poor legs tremble. Sometimes they would just give out and down she would tumble. One of these days, she would break something and then she'd be done for. She snorted. As if she wasn't done for now!

"What is it like outside, Ah Sing?" she called to the houseboy over her shoulder. "Is it very warm? As if it ever gets really warm in this God-forsaken place! Shall I wear a wrap?"

"Shawl," Ah Sing advised her. He tucked her white merino shawl around her bony shoulders and, throwing open the door, led her down the front steps and along the flagstone path into the little cutting garden on the south side of the house, where he deposited her on a stone bench.

"I patterned this garden on my mother's," Lily explained to the Chinaman. "Such a beautiful garden. I hired a farmer to cart a wagon of soil up from Aylmer. Timmins is built on an esker, you see. All sand, useless for flowers. Useless for anything. Stony and barren . . ."

It was early June. The bulbs had sent forth tentative shoots — irises, daffodils, tulips and a few tender lilies. Later would come the other flowers — foxgloves and holly-hocks, columbines and sweetpeas — and, later still, zinnias and asters and Russian sunflowers as tall as the potting-shed roof.

Ah Sing knelt beside a cluster of stalks that bowed under the weight of green pods. Reaching out, he touched one lightly with the tip of a finger. No, he thought to him-self. Not quite ready.

Lily noted his apparent interest. "Poppies," she explained. "I planted them last year . . . before I became so ill."

Ah Sing nodded. "Ah Sing's family grow many poppies back in Yanping," he informed her. "Poppies very excellent flower."

"Very pretty, yes, " Lily agreed vaguely. An auger of white heat bored into the centre of her forehead, the beginning of a headache that would spread — it was the sunlight, intense after she'd spent so long indoors. "I should have worn a hat," she observed.

"Ah Sing get hat," the houseboy promptly offered.

"No, no, I'll go inside. It's the light. So bright." The familiar, dank pain was beating behind her eyes like a second straining heart, while her true heart burgeoned into a huge millstone, taking up too much room in her torso, crowding out her poor lungs, making it difficult to breathe. She gasped for air and laughed. "Oh, but I'm like a bat these days, Ah Sing!" she wheezed. "Some wizened, squinting, nocturnal creature, fit for nothing but to hang by my feet from the rafters!"

"Ah Sing help missy up! You go inside now." Taking the physician's wife by both her elbows, the houseboy tugged Lily to her feet.

"Yes, thank you, Ah Sing," she began. "I feel so . . ." An image slipped through her mind, fleeting as a nurse that disappears down a darkened corridor at night — it was the memory of Edgar turning from the bed, bearing the last of her babies away in a tin basin, covered with a white linen napkin so that she couldn't glimpse the bloody misshapenness of it. Oh, but she had! She had! "Vertiginous," she concluded, swaying slightly.

Ah Sing steadied her. "When poppies bloom, missy feel better," he encouraged her, smiling and bobbing his head to underscore his conviction.

Lily smiled wanly and patted him on the shoulder. "Perhaps," she said, mindful that she was indulging her servant in a way that she would not have indulged her husband. But the houseboy was so simple. Childlike and guileless.

Every day the false Ah Sing checked the poppies in Lily Kirby's garden. As they matured, they came to resemble tiny crowned pumpkins: they hardened, developing raised ridges that ran from top to bottom. One morning, they looked as though they had been dusted with talcum powder. Two days later, he could just make out small black dots where the opium had oozed through pinprick holes; in addition, he could detect a slight acrid odour. As the week progressed, the odour grew stronger and sharper. Finally, on a Sunday morning while Dr. Kirby was attending Trinity Anglican Church and Lily was resting on her divan in the bedroom, Ah Sing vomited his meagre breakfast and developed a headache that lasted all day long. He knew then that quantities of opium were leaking through the disintegrating pods and tainting the air, that it was time to harvest the pods.

After waiting until a few minutes before midnight, when he could be certain that his master and mistress slept, the houseboy stole out to the garden. He would not need the coal-oil lamp to do his work, for the moon was almost full. A neighbour's dog, smelling the Chinaman on the wind, barked uproariously. Ah Sing froze where he was, halfway between the house and the potting shed. A back door opened, and the dog was sharply reprimanded and shooed inside. Ah Sing exhaled in sharp relief and proceeded to pick his way down the uneven flagstone path to the bed of nodding poppies.

Kneeling, he reached into the rolled-up sleeve of his tunic and extracted a razor blade, with which he made deft incisions in the pods. This was how his grandmother had taught him to harvest opium back in Yanping; his ancestors had been doing it this way since the time of the first ancestor, many centuries ago. Gently, he squeezed the black liquor from the lacerated pods into a little milk-glass bowl, careful to retain every drop. There were perhaps two dozen poppies in Lily's garden, enough to produce only a very small supply of opium, and so he could waste none. When he had milked all the pods, he crept back into the dark house to sleep a while before getting up at six o'clock to make the doctor his breakfast.

Over the next week, Ah Sing processed the opium. For one day, he macerated the liquor in rainwater, which he ladled out of the rain barrel. Next, he strained the opium through flannel, reduced the residue to a uniform pulp with the back of a fork, then macerated it again. He repeated this process three times. He set the pulp on the windowsill in the attic so it could dry out sufficiently to form pellets, which could be stored indefinitely, discreetly, before visiting the Chinese Tea and Herb Sanatorium, where he acquired a bag of lichee nuts, a tin of Tiger Balm, some pickled ginger, a pipe and a long needle, or *yen hok*.

Then he waited.

All day long, Lily Kirby had been complaining of headache and palpitations, of difficulty breathing and faintness.

Nevertheless, when the clock struck half past seven that evening, Dr. Kirby stood before the mirror in the front hall, straightening his tie and adjusting his westcott in preparation for poker night at the Empire Hotel — Dr. Kirby never missed poker night.

"Don't wait up for me," he called up the stairs to his wife. "I'll be late, as usual."

To Ah Sing, he murmured, "She's angry at me for going out. Oh, I can tell. Well, I can't be expected to stay in every night, now can I? Keep an eye on her for me, won't you, Ah Sing?"

"Oh, very good, sir," the houseboy said, nodding vigorously to indicate he understood the injunction. "Ah Sing take good care of missy."

"Excellent chappy," Dr. Kirby commended him absently, patting his waistcoat pockets to check for his billfold, pocket watch and keys. "Damned if I know what's wrong with her. Up here, if you ask me." He tapped the side of his head. "Well, then, I'm off."

Ah Sing brought Lily her dinner on a tray — a poached egg on toast, tea with a quadrant of lemon. "Ah Sing bring missy something make pain go away," he informed her as he settled her with her tray, adjusting her pillows, smoothing her coverlet.

"Nonsense," replied Lily. She poked tentatively at the congealed egg yolk with her silver fork, eyeing it as if she didn't quite know what it was. "What have you brought me?"

"Old Chinese medicine," Ah Sing told her. "Ah Sing make special for missy."

"Oh, no you don't, Ah Sing!" Lily exclaimed. She returned her fork to the tray without breaking the yolk.

"I've heard all about the strange things you people eat — eels and bird's nests!"

"No eels. No bird's nests," Ah Sing assured her. "And you don't eat it, Missy. You smoke it. I made it from your poppies, the poppies in the garden. Here. Missy eat egg now for Ah Sing. Egg very good for missy." Taking the fork from the tray, he pierced the egg yolk and handed the plate and fork to Lily. "Eat," he encouraged her.

"You made . . . opium?" Lily gasped. "From my little Icelandic poppies?"

"Opium, yes," Ah Sing nodded. "Chinese call it joss."

"Opium!" Lily repeated, spreading the yolk over the surface of the toast with the back of the fork.

"My grandmother taught me how. Joss very good. You like. Pain go away. *Pouf!*"

"I . . . I couldn't possibly smoke opium," Lily demurred, cutting off a corner of the egg-soaked toast and placing it in her mouth. She chewed. Of course she had heard all about opium dens, dark cellars lined with bamboo racks that cost two bits to enter and were inhabited by hollow-eyed coolies. Indeed, she had heard rumours that certain ladies of her acquaintance had been known to frequent such establishments. A great scandal, of course. Still, they had yet to forfeit their place in society. "Well, perhaps I could try a little," she conceded. "The pain is, after all, unendurable. Like broken glass around my heart. But no one must know, Ah Sing."

"Oh no, missy."

"Particularly not my husband."

"Ah Sing never tell Dr. Kirby."

"All right, then," she said, and pushing the tray away,

she sat up on the divan, folding her hands primly on her lap. "I'll try some. What could it hurt?"

Ah Sing fetched from his pantry a pellet of opium, the pipe and needle that he had secured from the Chinese Tea and Herb Sanatorium, and a candle jammed into a tarnished brass candlestick, then he returned to the bedroom. "Missy lie on couch," he advised her. "Head on pillow. Very comfortable."

Lily reclined on her side, her head supported by the satin bolster.

Ah Sing lit the candle, skewered the bead of opium on the needle, which was the length of a hatpin, and held it over the candle's flame until it became somewhat malleable. Then he thrust it into the hole of the pipe and, holding the bead in place with two fingers, drew the needle from it. He gave the pipe to Lily. "Suck on pipe, missy. Deep, deep. Then hold breath. Long as you can."

It crept over her like a cloud — gently, silently, rounding and smoothing all the rough edges. And there were so many rough edges, so many points on which her existence snagged and hung her up. Now Lily's bone marrow began to tingle. She glowed like a mercury lamp in the deep opium fog, feeling strangely relaxed, yet also energetic. All her pain was gone, soaked up as if with a sponge and then put away from her in some basin somewhere. She had never felt so free, so exquisitely . . . comfortable. Lily closed her eyes. Space swelled, seemed to descend into chasms and sunless abysses. She floated downwards.

When she opened her eyes again, it was to see Ah Sing kneeling by her side like some sort of Oriental cupbearer. What was he saying to her? She couldn't make it out. Ah! But of course! He was speaking Chinese. Odd that she had never before heard him speak his own language. Lily listened intently — her ears rang, her hearing had become, all of a sudden, acute. His speech was low, rapid, earnest, a jumble of dissonances and discordances.

"What?" she croaked.

"Ah Sing tell story of first poppy," Ah Sing informed her. "Long time ago, there was a beautiful lady who smelled so bad nobody would marry her. Very sad. When she died, a poppy grew from her grave."

Imagine! What a curious story! But by now, Lily had turned another corner in the labyrinth that her thought processes had become. Ah Sing is as fluent in his language as I am in mine! she realized. Why had she not thought of this before? Because of his broken English, she had always thought of him as halfwitted, but doubtless a celestial would think the same of her were she to try to speak Mandarin. She looked at her servant, astounded by a complexity of character and breadth of experience that she had never before associated with the slight Chinaman.

In fact, all of a sudden, there was so much Lily understood. It was as if all knowledge were opening up for her like a big book. Only everything was happening so fast that she had no time to decide which of a thousand things to think about first. For example, if she were to ask Ah Sing to speak Chinese again, she was convinced that it would be just a matter of minutes before she could decipher his peculiar language. What is more, she was absolutely certain that she would now be able to unravel mysteries that had previously eluded her, such as how the Holy Ghost progresses from the Father and the Son and how the Eucharist becomes the body and the blood of Christ. Not to mention gravity, the procession of the equinoxes, and yes, even algebra.

She noticed with a start that Ah Sing had left the bedroom. Now, suddenly, he returned, looming. He was carrying a beautiful little blue box. "Missy want sweet?" he asked.

"A sweet?" she managed. Why not? she thought, she who for months had taken nothing but a boiled egg, toast, broth and tea was suddenly ravenous for a sweet. "Yes, please, Ah Sing! A sweet!"

He fed her the hot, sugared ginger piece by piece. She ate greedily but declined the last piece. "For you," she whispered. "And . . . some joss too. For you."

So Ah Sing descended the stairs to the pantry for a second pip of opium. When he returned to the bedroom, however, Lily failed to acknowledge his presence. She lay on the divan, on her side, with her knees drawn up slightly and her hands folded over her breast. Her eyes were closed and her breath came at regular intervals, deep and rhythmic. Not sleeping, he thought, but dreaming. By now, the physician's wife would be far, far away. The houseboy draped a silken piano shawl over her, turned out the light, and set the pipe, needle and candlestick on her dinner tray, carrying it downstairs. Later, after he had tidied up the kitchen, he withdrew into his little pantry to smoke the pip of opium.

Dr. Kirby, on returning home from the Empire Hotel just past one o'clock in the morning, not precisely sober yet not too confoundedly drunk to notice, observed the great calmness that pervaded that troubled dwelling and thought, upon seeing his wife dreaming on her divan in the moonlight, that he had never seen her look so lovely or so peaceful.

The three little Cornish boys hung over the fence, taunting Ah Sing as he knelt beside the new flowerbed behind the garden shed. Their clothes were dirty and their faces smudged with coal.

> *Chinkee Chinkee Chinaman, sitting on a fence.*
> *Try to make a dollar out of fifteen cents!*
> *Chinkee Chinkee Chinaman, sitting on a rail.*
> *Along comes a white man and snips off his tail!*

"May you be dismembered and eaten alive by a terrible *iau-kuai!*" Ah Sing cursed them.

"*Chinna-mucka-hyoo!*" the boys retaliated, hurling lumps of purloined coal at the houseboy before shrieking with laughter and fleeing.

"May the White Tiger and the Azure Dragon abandon the grave of your grandmother," yelled the furious Ah Sing. "May she rise from her grave to haunt you!"

Containing his anger with some difficulty, the paper son began to etch into the upturned earth with a trowel furrows in which to plant the package of poppy seeds. "Barbarians!" he muttered under his breath. "Savages!"

When the first snow fell in October, Ah Sing, realizing that he could no longer grow the poppies he needed for Lily's opium, made some discreet inquiries of his former employer, Du Quong, whose brother ran a joss house in the Moneta area, down towards the river. From that point on, the house-boy made regular weekly pickups at the joss house, for by now Lily could not do without the opium for even a day before all her symptoms became much worse and she began to weep and rant and complain of aching in her legs and sounds booming and echoing in her head. "The House of Blue Mirrors," she called it. "A terrible funhouse place."

Dr. Kirby was spending more and more time away from the house. He had a busy practice, and now that Lily no longer complained about how often he went out or how late he stayed, he found himself in great demand at the lodge or the hotel.

"I cannot believe the change in her," he told Ah Sing. "She seems so calm. Patient and kind. Well, she wasn't that way before, I tell you! Always fretting over some damn thing! It's as if nothing bothers her any more. It's a great relief, by George, though I do wonder at her otherworldliness. Does she not seem . . . removed to you?"

"What, master, sir?" Ah Sing asked, blinking.

"Oh! What am I saying?" Dr. Kirby laughed, slapping the houseboy on the back. "Just thinking aloud."

About this time, a great deal of anti-Chinese sentiment was stirred up by the newspaper, acting in conjunction with one of its principal advertisers, the Sanitary Steam Laundry, a facility operated by a Mr. George Smythe and in competition with Du Quong.

"Chinese coolies are leprous in blood and unclean in habit," the editor of the newspaper advised the citizens of Timmins. "Chinese laundries are just fronts for white slavery and opium smuggling," Mr. Smythe told anyone who would listen. So many people believed him that, notwithstanding the fact that no females had yet to go missing from the area, white girls were prohibited from waiting tables in Chinese restaurants. "Otherwise the moon-eyed celestials will dope them with opium, lock them in wicker baskets and export them under the cover of darkness to far-eastern ports, where they will be subjected to such degradation as would make a Christian weep and tear his hair!" warned the newspaper.

"Stuff and nonsense!" retorted Dr. Kirby, thumping his rolled-up newspaper against his knee. "Prejudice and ignorance! Why, I myself have a Chinese houseboy, and I don't mind telling you that I think the world of him. As for my wife, she finds him completely indispensable."

After seven years in Timmins and scrupulous frugality, Ah Sing managed to save $2,700 — more than enough money to return to Yanping in silken robes.

"Spring comes, Ah Sing go home," the houseboy advised Lily Kirby. It was ten-thirty on a cold December morning. The garden outside was blanketed in five feet of snow — it reached almost to the eaves of the potting shed. The paper son spoke casually, as if in passing. He hoped that Lily would take the news equally casually.

Instead, she seized his arm. "What?" Lily gasped. "Leave me? Oh, but, Ah Sing, whatever would I do without you? I have grown so fond of you and . . . who would bring me my medicine? No! No!" She burst into noisy tears. "It's out of the question."

Ah Sing struggled to maintain his composure; it would not do to let Lily see how agitated he was. He had accomplished all that he had set out to do in this wilderness peopled by savages, and he had paid a huge price for what he would bear away with him. This foreign woman would not stop him from returning to his civilized country. "Not worry, missy," he reassured Lily. "Ah Sing talk to brother of Du Quong. Much joss. Send boy every day."

"But you are so discreet, Ah Sing," Lily argued. "Oh, get me a handkerchief, will you? I'm all soggy. You have no right to upset me so!"

Ah Sing selected a handkerchief from the stack in the top drawer of the oak bureau and handed it to the physician's wife. It had her initials embroidered on it — L.K. — and a cluster of forget-me-nots.

She dabbed at her eyes, sniffled, then blew her nose. "It's a matter of trust," she explained. "You see, I can trust you. But this Du Quong and his brother . . . this boy he would send . . . How do I know they can keep a secret?"

A secret all of Chinatown has known for the past seven years, Ah Sing thought. He said, "Brother of Du Quong no talk. Boy no talk either. Talking very bad for business. Missy's secret safe with Du Quong's brother."

She sunk back onto her divan, closing her eyes. "No. I'm determined. You shan't go. I won't let you. If you try, I shall stop you. I shall tell the police that you steal from me, have stolen from me all along. Silver. Jewellery. I will hide the silver and the jewellery somewhere no one will ever find it. That locket of my mother's. Old Mrs. Kirby's rubies and my pearls. Somewhere. Perhaps in the attic or near the potting shed. Then you'll be deported back to China, all right, but you will have to forfeit your ill-gotten savings. Oh, yes! And then what would be the point of returning? No, Ah Sing, you must stay where you are needed at least for the present. Later, perhaps, you may go."

Ah Sing paid a visit to the Chinese Tea and Herb Sanatorium, a dank and crowded little establishment at the corner of Birch and Third. Depending on what the proprietor, Pung Kee, could finagle by way of merchandise, the sanatorium sold everything from bitter melon, Chinese cabbage, and Peking ducks preserved in jelly to rhino-horn aphrodisiacs, powdered deerhorn, and potions of pickled wildcat, chicken and snake. In one corner of the store teetered a stack of yellow lacquered coffins — the store's backroom served the local Chinese community as a dead house where the bones of those unfortunate enough to die in Timmins could lay for seven years before they were shipped back to China.

Ah Sing was determined that his bones should not suffer this dire fate.

"I need a poison," he informed Pung Kee.

Dr. Kirby sat slumped on the sofa in the sitting room, staring straight ahead, a teacup balanced on one knee. The funeral guests had gone now. They had come for Edgar's sake, all those kind-hearted, sympathetic guests: the ladies at whose pleasant, well-appointed homes he played bridge; the lawyers and politicians with whom he played poker at the Empire or, on Thursdays, billiards; the tradesmen and merchants with whom he threw darts at the Moneta. No one had really known his wife. She had had no friends. To the townspeople's recollection, she had always been sickly, although rumours had begun to percolate through the household servants that there were other reasons for Lily Kirby's reclusive ways.

"I would do an autopsy," Dr. Kirby told Ah Sing now — the houseboy was busy cleaning up after the guests — "but really, what would be the point? I'm certain it was stomach cancer. The vomiting and the pain . . . the convulsions towards the end. What else could it be? And of course, it was a long time in the coming. At least — I don't know — six . . . nine months since she began to complain of the nausea and the difficulty breathing?"

"Long time," Ah Sing confirmed, carefully piling teacups onto a tray.

"Poor sweet Lily," Dr. Kirby muttered, shaking his head. He handed Ah Sing the teacup on his knee and, standing stiffly, walked into the dining room. He poured himself a shot of whisky from the crystal decanter on the buffet, drank it back and poured himself another before sitting at the oval oak table. "When I first met her down at Alma College there in St. Thomas, she was so full of life. Would you believe it, Ah Sing? She was almost plump! And rosy. Such a beautiful woman and as happy as a lark. I should never have brought her here. The cold blighted her like it will blight any rose. Being away from her family . . . And the babies. Did you know she lost three babies, Ah Sing?

"Yes, Doctor," Ah Sing replied. "Missy tell me babies die."

"Well, I don't know if you could call them babies exactly!" Dr. Kirby snorted. "Misshapen messes is more like it. Blood puddings." Standing once again, the physician crossed to the buffet and brought the decanter of whisky back with him to the table. He poured himself another shot. "Well, regardless," he continued, "each of those still-births seemed to drain that much more life out of her. When I think back on it, I realize she had been wasting away for the past eight years or so. Growing thinner, more distant and remote. Living in her own world. Sometimes I would come into her room and she would look at me with these vacant eyes, as though she didn't recognize me, as though she couldn't quite remember just who it was I was. Her eyes . . . It was as if she walked with ghosts or some-thing." Dr. Kirby shook his head again. "I can't say I'll miss her," he said. "What was there to miss?"

A few weeks after the funeral, the false Ah Sing informed Dr. Kirby that he would be returning to China but had found an excellent houseboy to replace him — another paper son from the Four Districts by the name of Ah Foo.

"Fine! Fine!" said Dr. Kirby distractedly. He was late for

an appointment. "Good man, Ah Sing. Damned shame to lose you. Lily would have been upset. Glad you waited."

That evening, Ah Sing threw what was left of the arsenic that Pung Kee had sold him almost a year before onto the grate in the sitting-room fireplace and set fire to it. It gave off an odour like garlic before dissolving into a fine ash that dusted the bottom of the fireplace.

Tai Soong, previously known as Ah Sing, returned to Yanping with more than three thousand Canadian dollars — he had managed to save even more in the period that intervened between Lily's refusal to allow him to leave and her death. By the standards of the Four Districts, he was now a wealthy man. Accordingly, the authorities promptly made him a magistrate, and thereby, even wealthier. Tai Soong built a house for the wife he had married shortly after his return from Canada; she was to bear him, in time, six children, all of whom would live and four of whom would be boys. The house was very much in the Chinese style, encircled by a brick wall and roofed with glazed tiles. Just as Tai Soong had hoped, it was filled with porcelain pots and fishbowls and carvings in jade and ivory. He had many servants and was much sought out as an old man for his account of his sojourn abroad.

"Going to Canada is like going to the moon," he would tell his rapt listeners. "White and cold . . . and the barbarity of the inhabitants is such that it can scarcely be described in words."

THE BOCKLES

For three hundred years, Pulglases had worked the South Crofty mine, which lies between Camborne and Redruth on the Connor, or the Red River, so called because of the residue of tin that washes down from the mine and turns the water a rusty colour before it dumps it into St. Ives Bay. And before the tinners went underground, Pulglases streamed for ore in that same region, down there towards the south of the County of Cornwall and inland, on the road between Truro and Penzance. South Crofty was a deep mine: four hundred fathoms blasted through hard granite. Not that this was unusual. All the mines in Cornwall were deep, for the ore is borne in fissures running vertically through the rock, and each of these fissures must be shafted separately if it is to be worked. The tin they mined in South Crofty was sweetness itself, like moon parings, but it didn't dig easy. The deeper they drilled, the more water seeped into the shaft, for saving that short piece of land north of the Tamar, Cornwall is an island, afloat in the Atlantic like a boat. So the South Crofty miners worked a donkey-powered rag and a chain operation to de-water the mine, and that was a job to which Pulglases took — driving the donkey and, later, working the pump in the engine house — with the result that, as long as anyone could remember, a Pulglase had been in charge of drying the shaft while other, lesser Pulglases had worked deep in the mine, drilling and mucking or working the 303 machine.

There was something that set the Pulglases apart from other folk. Way back, a Pulglase man had married a changeling (for piskies, like mockingbirds, are wont to creep into a mortal's house by night and abscond with whatever babies they can lay their hands on, leaving one of their own very peculiar offspring in their stead — and these changelings are not only odd-looking, but also difficult to keep clothed, as piskies prefer to rush around buck naked in all kinds of weather, with only their long hair for a covering). From that union on, not only were the Pulglases short-legged, but they also possessed the ability to converse with piskies. Moreover, though it made for a draught, they built their houses of granite or greenstone with holes strategically placed in the walls so that the piskies could enter and leave at will. "To bar them from the hearth would be to drive away good luck," they explained to dubious neighbours. Still, it had to be admitted that the Pulglases had no need to place those knobs of lead known as piskies' paws on the roofs of their houses to prevent the piskies from dancing on them and thereby souring the milk, and that as a family, they tended to thrive, living longer lives than most and their children scarcely ever dying, provided the child was not born at the interval between the old and new moons and its head was not washed before the requisite twelve months specified by those wise in these matters.

Now it happened that there were bockles in the South Crofty mine — bockles or knackers, it was unclear which. Knackers are the spirits of tinners who died unexpectedly in underground accidents. They are malevolent-looking — gnarled, with oversized heads, squinting eyes and mouths that stretch from ear to ear. They stand no taller than three feet and have long grey beards. Bockles, on the other hand, are that breed of pisky that lives underground. No matter what level of South Crofty a miner was working on, he could hear piskies knocking at the rock from some nearby point within the earth with little picks and axes and hammers — sometimes a tinner would even uncover some child-sized tool hidden away in a rock cranny — but just where they were digging was impossible to make out. Moreover, the sound was most clearly discerned at the very deepest part of the shaft. This led the miners to conclude that somewhere a way far down lay a rich lode, for it is a well-known fact that both knackers and bockles can actually smell copper, tin and silver the way a man can smell his dinner as he comes over the moor towards home. However, everyone was afraid to stray into such unfamiliar territory — there was no telling what reception they might get. Knackers are almost always cantankerous, and piskies are, at best, capricious, friendly one moment and devilish the next. Everyone, that is, except for Kevern Pulglase, who maintained the pumps at the engine house as his father had before him, and his son, Digory, just turned seventeen and in charge of clearing the gutters that ran along the train track inside the mine.

Now Kevern, in his time, had been an inquisitive boy and quick, or so his teachers had said before he quit school at the age of nine to work underground. He was always poking about by himself amid the scrub and gorse on the moor, trapping rabbits for his mother and shooting plover and woodcock to take home, and so he had come to have some direct experience of piskies, having encountered them a number of times and observed their dances. That, plus, of course, his pisky blood. His son, Digory, on the other hand, was a thick sort of boy, loutish and slow. Like all the Pulglases, he had short, bowed legs, big ears and a long, pulled face. Like those in his mother's family, he was rheumy, weak-eyed and tended to leak at the nose. The most interesting thing Digory had done to date was to overturn his friend Jacca's backhouse when Jacca's uncle Ythel was in it. As for piskies, Digory had never knowingly encountered one, though his nan had often told him that she had seen them dance round his head as an infant. "That could be a good thing . . . or a bad one," she advised him. (Digory's nan could cure warts, pox, whooping cough and hernias and so was widely sought after as a charmer.)

"We'll fetch us out tonight," his father told him one fair midsummer's Saturday, "and see what we can see. It's a full moon, and that's a favoured time for pisky-spotting. If they be bockles and not knackers, they'll be out tonight. But listen to me, son — you cannot breathe a word of this to anyone. Not to your nan or your ma or that Jacca fellow or that Loveday lass you've been courting, with the mouth on her like an open trap. And especially not to the boys on your shift or any miner at South Crofty. For if my plan succeeds, we'll make of ourselves rich men, but t'will be at the expense of the others, and they won't like us too well if they know what we're up to. So can you keep a tight lid on it, lad?"

"Why, yes, Da," Digory replied, uncomprehending.

Accordingly, father and son left their house, which was on the main road leading out of Redruth, just as the moon was rising over the hill. In Kevern's packsack were a couple of pasties, sticks of yellow and black barley and two Mason jars of that Cornish mead made from clear honey and seasoned with root ginger and rosemary (this was on account of it being the full Mead Moon). They sat down under a yew tree outside the entrance of the South Crofty and waited. Sure enough, just after midnight, a whole pack of bockles came swarming out of the mine's entrance, dragging bags twice their size behind them — Kevern saw at once that they were bockles and not knackers because of the likeness they bore to moor piskies. These bags the bockles carried off to a place about a mile north of town on the moor's edge, with Digory and Kevern scrambling through the bracken and bramble behind them. There, beside a quaking pool edged with lady's smock and ragged robin, they spilled the big sacks onto the dewy sedge to make a pile of shining ore, which they proceeded (being piskies) to dance merrily about. Kevern and Digory, somewhat fuddled by drink by this time, secreted themselves behind an outcrop of weathered, lichenous granite to watch. "Would you look at that!" Digory exclaimed to his father under his breath. "They're as small as my . . ." He paused in consternation, for when it came down to it, he couldn't say how small the bockles actually were. And this was quite to be expected, for although piskies give the impression of being very small folk, it is impossible to say whether they are this big or that big because 1) they tend to fluctuate in size; 2) they gutter and flicker like candles in a wind; and 3) most people who see them are at least a little drunk.

In the case of bockles, they are earthen in hue, stained brown with mossy undertones. They are slight of build, boneless in appearance and go about entirely naked except that their long, tangled hair reaches frequently to their knees, concealing such private parts as they possess. They emit the slightest phosphorescent glow, smell of honeysuckle after a rain, and when they speak or sing, there is a peculiar resonance to the sound, as if the listener's ears were ringing. Those who encounter them frequently experience vertigo.

"Whoa!" muttered Digory, clinging to the rock for support, for he suddenly felt dizzy and not a little nauseous.

"Stay here and keep quiet," his father advised him. Then, to Digory's amazement and somewhat to his alarm, Kevern squared his shoulders, took a deep breath and stepped out from behind the rock into the spill of moonlight and the very midst of the frolicking bockles. The piskies froze. Then one of them, a little taller than the others and having about him a somewhat regal air, said something to the rest in a slippery-eel voice the meaning of which Digory could almost but not quite grasp. All the bockles laughed and clapped their little hands — their laughter sounded like silver bells, their clapping like dry seed pods crushed by little feet.

"We meet again, cousin," the head of the bockles continued, turning back to Digory's father. "Only you are somewhat more gigantic than before. What is it you want from the bockles?"

"That's a lot of ore you have there, cousin!" observed Kevern. "You must have worked hard to break up so much with your little hammers."

"You know how we bockles like pretty things," replied the pisky. "Things that glitter and shine."

"I remember," Kevern assured him. "So I was thinking that we might make a deal."

The bockles murmured. A twittering sound like birds make in the rain.

"What kind of deal?" inquired the head bockle shrewdly.

"You tell me where to dig for the ore, and I and my son will bring you a tenth of the richest ore we find, properly dressed, so that you won't even have the trouble of breaking it up," offered Kevern.

"Is that your son standing over there behind that rock?"

"Yes," Kevern admitted.

"Let him stand up so the bockles may see his face."

"Digory, stand up!"

Digory shuffled to his feet, cap in hand, gulping.

The head bockle gazed at him intently and stroked his little chin. "Hmmmm . . ." he murmured.

"We can bring it here, to this very place, if you like." Kevern sweetened the deal.

"Aha!" The bockle considered the offer.

"It will give you more time to dance," Digory blurted out.

"Digory!" his father warned him.

"The boy makes a good point." The bockle interceded on Digory's behalf. "Very well, then. You will bring us the ore on the night of the full moon. A new load every full moon. Those are our terms."

"You have my word on it," Kevern swore.

"We'll have more than that if you are forsworn," the bockle reminded him, glancing at Digory.

Kevern nodded. "I know," he said. "I do not make this promise lightly. I know the consequences of failing to comply with the terms of a deal struck with piskies."

"I know you do," acknowledged the bockle. "My auntie, your nan, taught you well. We shall accept your offer. Go down into the mine tomorrow, when everyone else is at church. Go down to the very deepest level, where there is standing water. Listen carefully. I, on my side, shall strike my hammer against the rock three times. Dig in that spot and you will not be disappointed."

"I will do as you say," replied Kevern. "We shall both benefit from this arrangement. You will see."

"That we shall," concluded the bockle, turning back to the dance.

"We shall be rich men!" Kevern told his son excitedly as they stumbled back to their village. But Digory was so confounded by drink and the actual physical effect that the bockles have upon mortals (not only did he have less pisky blood than his father, but his body weight was also less) that he remembered the encounter as one would a peculiarly compelling dream — vividly, but in snatches and blurts.

From that day on, for the next seven years, the Pulglases, father and son, crept down to the mine of a Sunday morning, just as the bells of the little Wesleyan chapel were beginning to call folks into church and dug wherever the bockles' hammers directed them. One tenth of the broken-up and dressed ore Kevern set out for the bockles on the night of the full moon; the other nine-tenths he sold to a man who traded in black-market ore. As Kevern had predicted, the Pulglases became wealthy men in this way, able to buy a farm in the country and pigs and sheep and to build a fine stone house on their land, with holes worked right into the walls for the piskies to come and go at will and full of all sorts of exotic treasures — a Royal Doulton figurine of a French lady on the mantelpiece, a tea caddy that came straight from India and an engraving of Dick Turpin on horseback that had once belonged to the local gentry. Kevern's mother and wife had not only a vegetable garden for growing parsnips, carrots and turnips, but also a cutting garden that Digory's mother planted with wallflowers and Canterbury bells. A hired boy cut pukes of turf and faggots of furze and kept their turbary filled to the top, and a girl from the neighbouring farm helped out with the cooking. As for food, the Pulglases wanted for nothing. There was always a ham hock in the boil, or a fat roast of beef dripping with suet, or a big fish brought up from Gwithian wrapped in newspaper and lambasted with butter and then dredged in vinegar to be eaten with mustard.

Indeed, the Pulglases became so prosperous that no one could figure out why they continued to work in the mine. "It's in our blood," Kevern explained. "The Pulglases have always been tinners." The truth was that they had not yet grown quite rich enough to quit and so kept on postponing their retirement, for at that time, they would lose access to their underground treasure.

One day, when Kevern was riding the hoist down to the bottom of the mine to check the water level (for they had recently drilled down an additional twenty-six feet and experienced a bad run of flooding as a result), the rod snapped. Kevern and thirty other men hurtled to their deaths

2,400 feet below. Digory had just ridden the hoist up a few moments before and was in the punch room clocking out from his shift. The sound of the men screaming as they fell was muted by the roar of the drills from below and the noisy suck of the big pump. It sounded distant, wadded up like a piece of paper, unconnected to his life and experience. The mine was closed for three days while they removed the bodies, which were little more than pulp and were unrecognizable. "Like straining a stew," as one miner on the burial detail commented.

Digory was on his own.

Now, there were never two more different men than Digory Pulglase and his father. Kevern Pulglase was smart; Digory was stupid. Kevern was prudently cautious; Digory, careless and feckless. The first full moon after his father died, Digory delivered a tenth of his spoils to the bockles as usual, but the next full moon after that, he skimmed a little off the top of the tenth, figuring that the bockles would not notice the slight discrepancy. Every full moon for a year thereafter, he skimmed a little bit more and a little bit more off the piskies' portion until finally, at the rising of the Blood Moon in October (so called for pig-sticking), he got so drunk down at Davy Jones's Locker that he forgot to leave the bockles their tithe at all. When the milk did not sour in the days that followed and the baby's first tooth did not come in snaggled — by this time, Digory had married his lumpish sweetheart, Loveday Carvyth, and had two great walloping sons on her — he figured that either the bockles didn't care about the bargain he had failed to keep or, very possibly, their power was less than his father had imagined. He even began to wonder if the bockles existed at all. Perhaps the mead had caused him to see things that weren't there — mead could do that if left too long in the fermenting.

The Snow Moon came and went, then the Oak Moon. Again Digory got drunk at the pub and did not leave the bockles their tithe. No harm befell him or his family. That Sunday, however, when he had descended deep into the mine, as was his wont, there was no bockle hammer to tell him where to dig. He sat there in the cold, quaky dark on an empty carbide tin for two hours, but the bockles did not signal him. "Well, that's that," he said to himself and the next day retired from the mine and went up village to live on his farm.

A whole half-year came and went. Then, in July, on the Mead Moon, the same moon that had shone when Kevern and Digory had made their original pact with the bockles, Digory celebrated by riding his bicycle into Redruth and closing the pub there some seven hours later. With no thought of piskies, he made his weaving way home – five miles up and down narrow roads through the moon-bathed countryside – to discover that his fine stone house had fallen into a hole twice its size and one and a half storeys deep.

Apparently, his father had built it over some mine workings abandoned so long before that no one had remembered exactly where they were located, and the ground had finally given way under the immense weight. Everyone who had been inside the house when the cave-in occurred died, of course, buried in a heap of square granite blocks and heavy oaken beams — this included Digory's wife, his two babies, his mother and an as-yet-unmarried sister. The only survivors were his dog, Alfie, who had been asleep in the barn at the time, and his old nan, his father's mother, who had been availing herself of the backhouse when the ground stove in. "A terrible rumbling, like the earth was opening up to let the dead rise up," was how she described it. "Then the most fearful silence. Oh, I should have known it was coming when I heard the owl hoot and then that hen of your ma's actually crowing." Later she tried to comfort her distraught grandson. "It was not your fault, boy," she told him. "Nor your father's neither. Who was to know there was a great bloody hole under the house?" But Digory knew full well that it was his fault, that the bockles were punishing him for not keeping his part of the bargain struck on that long-ago night. He had been a fool to think that they had not noticed or did not care. He had been a fool to think them powerless or — more foolish still — non-existent. Digory was convinced that the bockles had either dug the hole under the house or, more likely, used their pisky powers to induce Kevern to build on that very spot, in case they should at some point require easy access to retribution.

Digory took to drink — that is, he took to drink more than he had previously taken to drink. Over the space of a year, he lost everything his father and he had acquired as a result of their deal with the bockles. The sheep died of giddie, the hogs of mumps and the horse of staggers. The corn took a mould on it and withered in the fields. Once again he was compelled to take up lodgings in Redruth and seek employment at the South Crofty mine. However, it was not the same as it had once been down in the shaft. The other men kept their distance, even his old friend Jacca, for if good luck had a tendency to rub off, bad luck was downright contagious. No man in his right mind wanted Digory on his shift or in the hoist bucket with him, for fear of cave-ins or missed holes or snapped cables. So Digory moved his nan into her sister's cottage and went west to Penwith, near Cape Cornwall, where he signed on to work at the Botallack mine. The Botallack's engine house was set high on a peak of granite overlooking the Atlantic, the ocean foaming at its base. The mine's underground workings extended out under the seabed, several fathoms deep. Digory was not used to working with the weight of the sea squeezing the rock over his head, making it creak and buckle. It was hot down the shaft and the air was leaden with heavy moisture — a man had to gulp for air and then strain his lungs just to breathe it. The roar of the waves breaking against the cliffs above him rang in his ears, making him dizzy, and salt water seeped into the rock crannies where he worked and clung to him like spray.

About this time, an agent in the employ of the Hollinger mine arrived at the Pomery Hotel in nearby St. Just — Colonel Putherbough, formerly of His Majesty's Army in India. Colonel Putherbough was an avuncular sort of man, lionine in aspect, with a big, well-made head and a mane of bright white hair; his manner was simultaneously hearty and smooth. He had been charged with recruiting as many Cornish tin and copper miners as he could muster, for skilled miners were at a premium in the Porcupine region of Northern Ontario, where the Hollinger was located, the frontier region being populated, in so far as it was populated, by feral French trappers, red Indians and what Cornishmen call woosers, wild men of the wood. Colonel Putherbough rented a hall and posted a notice, inviting the miners to attend a lecture on a Thursday evening. Seventy miners attended — already there had been talk of the Botallack being mined out, of the need to move on.

"The Hollinger is the largest gold mine in the British Empire. Why, did you know that it has more than one hundred miles of underground tunnels?" Colonel Putherbough astounded his audience. "Last year alone, the Hollinger produced $68,000 of gold ore each and every month of the year! And easy to drill and blast. No fear of the ocean coming down on top of you if you hit a missed hole. No, sir. As for Canada . . . well, let me tell you, my friends, it's the most beautiful country in the world. Rugged. No doubt about that. And cold, I'll grant you, but bracing." He thumped his barrel chest, then coughed. "Not damp and drizzly as it is here." Taking a snowy white hanky from his pocket, he blew his nose loudly. "As for the wages! Eighty-five Canadian dollars a month . . . and that's before your bonus, gentlemen. Plus, if you have a wife or get yourself one, the company will give you a house of your very own."

Later, Digory travelled to Redruth to see his nan. "Would there be piskies in Canada?" he asked her.

She just shook her woolly grey head. "Not Cornish piskies, I shouldn't think," she averred. "Why do you ask?"

"Oh, naught," Digory reassured her hastily. Although in most matters, a loose-lipped man Digory had kept his word to his father in one respect — he had not breathed a word of their compact with the bockles to anyone. Nor was he about to break his promise now that he had gone and lost everything through his sloth and his greed; he could not bear for his nan, the only person left in the world who had any regard for him, to know that he was responsible for all their misfortune. "Would you come with me to Canada, then, Nan . . . if I decide to go?"

"Oh, no," Nan said, pouring her grandson a cup of tea

and dribbling condensed milk from the can into it. "Too old. I'm happy enough here with Great-Auntie Lowena."

So three months later, Digory Pulglase went to Padstow, where the air smelled of tar, rope, rusted chain and tidal water, and set sail for Canada on a ship called the *Restless*, with a letter of employment signed by Colonel Putherbough in his jacket pocket. He made landfall at the Port of Quebec, along with ninety-nine other Cornishmen sponsored by the Hollinger, and from there he travelled by rail to Toronto and from Toronto to Northern Ontario, arriving in Timmins at the peak of the blackfly season in 1922. The township was not ten years old and still resembled the rough camp that it had so recently been, despite the fact that it boasted all the amenities of a typical Ontario town its size — a piggery, a bakery, a dairy, a dry-goods store and a shoemaker's, an ice-cream parlour, two hotels, two theatres, a barber shop, a pool room, a feed store, a livery, a lockup, a newspaper of record (the *Porcupine Advance*) and a firehall. The streets ran with mud; there was no grass to be found anywhere, but only raw, upturned earth and patches of sedge, and where there wasn't new construction, there were stumps and stacks of wood haphazardly piled and heaps of refuse.

Digory put up at the Old Boston Hotel, a two-storey clapboard, ramshackle affair of a building piled up on the corner of Pine and Second. Despite its designation, it was really a sort of rooming house catering to bachelor miners. For sixty cents a day, he shared a bed with a mucker called Romanian John who stood six foot five, weighed in at well over 250 pounds, spoke little English and had fleas. Digory did not like sleeping with Romanian John. The only way around it was to find himself a wife, thereby qualifying for a Hollinger house.

This was easier said than done. As it turned out, there were not many women unspoken for in Northern Ontario. Not only could a man not afford to be choosy, he also could not afford to wait if and when an opportunity to snag a wife presented itself. That was how the Cornishman found himself proposing to Moira Flannery a mere half an hour after meeting her at the Moneta (the local blind pig) and moments before impregnating her in the heap of rubble out back of it (if, indeed, he was the father of her baby, which was a matter of some speculation). Moira was eighteen, just off the boat herself from Cork, a big, blowsy girl, all pink and white, with reddish hair that did not so much grow from her head as sizzle from it and snapping blue eyes. She was in the employ of a prominent local physician at the time, Dr. Kirby. A strict man, he let the housemaid go when she confessed to being pregnant, but he gave her a decent sum of money by way of severance, realizing that she would have need of it in her straitened circumstances. Later he discovered that the housemaid had pawned numerous pieces of family silver over the short term of her employment, as well as some expensive jewellery belonging to his wife, and pocketed the money. When the physician threatened to call the constable, Moira countered with threats of an intimate nature. Upon reflection, Dr. Kirby contented himself with redeeming the pawned goods and hiring a Chinese houseboy to replace the Irish girl.

No doubt about it: Moira Flannery was a cunning opportunist, as mendacious as she was spirited and as insolent as she was indolent. But all Digory saw was a plump young bride ... and a Hollinger house. The Hollinger houses were narrow, two-storey structures consisting, for the most part, of tarpaper tacked onto a wooden frame. They were a dark green in colour, trimmed with white, and all of them were exactly alike. If there was a thing that could be counted upon, it was that no man would get a finer house than his fellow miner or a bigger one or even one that differed so much as one iota in its layout. On the first floor of a Hollinger house was a tiny parlour dominated by a tin stove — this parlour was so small that many a pregnant woman coming onto her time became stuck in it trying to turn around. There was also a kitchen that opened onto a lean-to. The second storey, where two small bedrooms crowded in under the eaves, was obtained by means of a precipitous flight of stairs. There were no halls or vestibules or mud rooms or even closets in a Hollinger house. These were considered superfluous luxuries. There was a sort of rough cellar that could serve a family as a cold room in which to store barrels of apples; sacks of potatoes, onions and turnips; old traps, fishlines and the like. They were cold, frail husks of houses compared with the fine, sturdy domicile his father had built back in Cornwall, but they were four walls a man could call his own, at least for the duration of his employment, and they were free. Moreover, Digory was lucky in that he put his name in at a time when the foundations of an entire block's worth of Hollinger houses had already been laid down on Borden Street. As soon as the ground thawed, miners working for extra dollars after their shifts underground would frame the houses and tack up the tarpaper and slap a roof on them in three weeks, and Digory and Moira would have their spanking new Hollinger house.

In the meantime, Digory rented a basement apartment that Moira had found for them down in the Young Street and Wilson Avenue area, not far from the Mattagami River. This was where their twin sons, Kevern and Elwyn, were born on a stormy February morning of that same year. These names, which Digory had picked out, were the very same as those borne by his and Loveday's sons. Needless to say, he did not tell Moira this . . . no, nor anything else about his first family and the terrible fate that had befallen them. He did not want her to think that he was unlucky or, worse (if she were to discover the real truth), stupidly venal. But who was there in this remote place to tell her? No one. Surely his secret was safe. He had been right to come so far away, to leave his guilty secret buried in a hole in Cornwall, mixed together with the blood and bones of his unfortunate family, dead through his fault, and therefore almost as if by his hand. For no matter how much Digory drank to forget, he had never forgotten this: that he had killed his mother and his sister, his wife and his sons as surely as if he had taken that old muzzle-loader down from over the mantlepiece and shot them, or lit a faggot of furze and hurled it through an open window into the sleeping house, or beaten their heads in with the back-side of a shovel. Now he began not so much to forget that he had killed them as to forget that they were dead in the first place. He did this consciously in the beginning, telling himself that the first Kevern and Elwyn had been reborn (in some ineffable way that he was hard put to understand but nevertheless felt certain was the case) in the identical bodies of their half-brothers. In addition, he took to calling Moira by his first wife's name: Loveday. "T'is a term of endearment," he reassured his new bride. "Like calling you darling or pet. For I love you all the day long." Not knowing that Loveday was, in fact, an old Cornish name, Moira took his pretty explanation at face value. As time wore on, the break between his old life and his new one knit up like a badly set bone, crooked and lumpy, but in its way intact. Cornwall and all that had passed there settled deeper into the mists that rolled across his mind, and there were times when he wondered if he and his father had ever made a compact with the bockles in the first place, and if what had befallen his family had taken place in reality or in a dream.

Moira did not share her husband's burgeoning sense of well-being. Being holed up in a dark and icy basement flat all day with two squalling babies and no money but what her poor dullard of a husband reluctantly doled out was not what she had had in mind when she travelled all the way across the Atlantic to Canada, then signed on to go to this remote frontier town. It was true that she had hoped to marry, but marry well. A rich man, an important man. Perhaps a prospector just off selling a rich claim. That was what she had wanted. That was what she had intended. And not only was Digory poor, with no prospects of being anything but poor, he was no prize either, with his big ears and his homely face and the start of a gut on him too, not to mention what he had for brains which, was what you did in the backhouse provided you could dig your way back there through all the snow. Moira had married Digory only because he had asked her, and because, of course, she was pregnant, though counting back, she was pretty sure that the twins weren't Digory's but belonged to that fellow who worked for the livery up on Third Street for a couple of months before heading west to Manitoba. Frenchy had been his name, or at least that was what he had told her. And that was another thing: it was not as if she had wanted children. She had been the oldest of twelve; sure but she had had her fill of mewling babies and snot-nosed toddlers back in County Cork. "If I never have to wipe another nose or bottom, I will be a happy woman," she had declared before bursting into tears. "How could I have let this happen to me? How? How?" But this story is not about Moira.

There's no gold camp in the world — nor any other camp where precious minerals are mined — without its high-graders. High-graders in Timmins were those who pocketed a few nuggets on a shift and then, stole, shaking in their boots, down to the Moneta to sell them to the man known far and wide as Père Henri. Père Henri was so short in stature that, had he been any shorter, he might have been considered a dwarf. He had a big, craggy head upon which was perched a black beret; small, squinty eyes that always appeared red and sore; a wide, mobile mouth; and a wispy grey goatee. Rumour had it that Père Henri had been a Catholic priest before he was defrocked, that he had come to this part of the North from Quebec to be a missionary to the Ojibwa but had somehow strayed. Certainly he effected a priest's collar, together with a priest's rusty black suit, and his manner was both solemn and sanctimonious. Père Henri always sat at a table in the back of the Moneta, right next to the rear door, to facilitate escape, should that prove necessary. It was his table. He sat in a special chair with an elevated seat that the blind pig's owner, Arthur McNab, had had made for him. McNab did not allow anyone else to sit there (Père Henri was good for business), and anyone who had been in Timmins for more than a fortnight knew better than to try, for if a miner was to earn that little bit extra, if he was to buy that new dress for his wife or those skates for his kids or a bicycle or a fiddle or a dogsled, his best recourse was Père Henri. Sinner though he undoubtedly was, the ex-clergyman always paid a fair price for gold.

At the time, Digory was on the night shift. One of the good things about being on the night shift was that a man could take more liberties during the hours of darkness than in the daylight, when there were not only more eyes to see what a body was up to, but also better visibility. Digory found that it was an easy thing to stroll up through one of the raises that opened out onto the golf course that Hollinger had built for its employees and toss a chunk of ore over the barbed-wire fence surrounding the compound. Later, after he had got off his shift, he would stroll over to that same fence, pocket the nugget and head home. The next evening, just before punching in, he would stop by the blind pig for a pint and conduct his business with Père Henri.

"You have a good eye for free gold, my friend," Père Henri complimented Digory. His smile was broad, his teeth green.

Digory shrugged but could not resist informing the high-grader, "I come by it naturally. My whole family . . . miners for generations."

"Mine too," Père Henri assured him smoothly. "For centuries."

It struck Digory then that Père Henri had a kind of mossy look to him that he found deeply suspicious. Perhaps it was because the room was smoky, or perhaps because he had begun to drink rather earlier than usual that day. That might account for the fact that the ex-priest seemed now to loom, now to shrink in his vision. He reminded Digory of someone. Just whom he could not quite remember, but the notion disturbed him at some fundamental level. He could not shake it, and from that time on, the Cornishman took his business elsewhere, selling his purloined nuggets to another entrepreneur, freshly arrived from the silver fields in Cobalt, despite the fact that this new high-grader consistently cheated him.

That year the thaw came much too quickly. In a matter of only ten short days, all the snow that had been shovelled up against the houses in the course of a long, hard winter and piled into banks as high as one-storey buildings and packed down on top of all the thoroughfares in town until street level stood three feet higher than it did in summer — all of this snow melted. The earth underneath people's feet turned sodden and spongy, and water levels soared in all the rivers and creeks and lakes of the district. The lower-lying areas along the river flooded to a depth of eighteen inches. Some houses in these areas listed tipsily. A barn collapsed into a heap of weathered lumber, then broke apart like a raft, boards spinning in the current, and an outhouse overturned and floated half way downstream before getting wedged in a culvert. Town Creek, which begins in northeast Timmins and meanders through large culverts to its outlet on the Mattagami River, not far from where the Mountjoy River joins the larger waterway, oozed and slopped over its banks. Things better left frozen unthawed — a winter's worth of odure, animal carcasses and viscera tossed out back of the butcher's shop or piggery to freeze in a heap, not to mention corpses kept in the undertaker's cold room until the earth could be worked with a shovel. Earthworms erupted from the soil in purplish pink handfuls, wild with joy, and the streets ran with thick, rank ooze. The *Porcupine Advance* had predicted rain that May 3, but no one was prepared for how much it would rain on that glowering, tempestuous day. During Digory's eight-hour shift alone, 6.7 inches fell.

The sudden increase in water levels, coupled with the blockage of Town Creek at several points owing to debris from previous flooding, caused a flash flood that overflowed the Mattagami's banks, ripping the wooden bridge from its moorings, collapsing corduroy roads and inundating the area of Wilson and Young with churning, muddy water. Digory stopped off at the Moneta for a pint before heading home, only to find McNab closing up early. The Scot was a bearishly big man with a curly russet beard streaked with white. He wore round wire spectacles and every second tooth in his head flashed gold. "Haven't you heard?" he asked Digory. "That whole area down by the river is flooded. Everybody's gone down to help. That's where I'm heading now. Say, don't you live down there yourself?"

"Wilson and Young," Digory confirmed.

"Well, I'd get home if I were you," McNab advised him, pulling on his mackintosh. "Père Henri was in here not a half-hour ago. Said Wilson was under two feet of water."

Suddenly, Digory felt dizzy. His stomach flipped over, blackness swam before his eyes and his knees buckled beneath him; he had to grab hold of McNab's arm to keep on his feet.

"Are you all right, Pulglase?" McNab snapped irritably. He was anxious to go.

"My wife and boys . . ." Digory gasped. The ringing in his ears and the rush of blood to his head was so loud that he could barely hear himself speak. "We're in a basement apartment. Just till they build our new Hollinger house. Jesus Christ! The basement! They'll drown like puppies in a barrel!"

"Like I said, man. You'd better get down there," said McNab, impatient to be gone himself. Then, when Digory continued to cling to his arm, sagging against him, he sighed with exasperation and offered, "Come on, then. We'll go together."

Taking Digory by the arm, the Scotsman hauled him outside and half dragged, half pushed him down the hill towards the river. It was hard going. The rain was steady in their faces, cold and hard, and the streets ran thick with slippery mud. Twice, Digory, who had yet to regain his equilibrium, pitched forward onto his hands and knees, only to have McNab haul him, streaming ooze and whimpering, roughly to his feet again and drive him forward like a farmer would a recalcitrant, disoriented beast. When they finally made it to the corner of Wilson and Young, it was just as Père Henri had said: the entire area was submerged under an expanse of brown, churning water that lapped up to the windowsills of the houses' first storeys. Together the two men waded through chest-high water out to a low barge onto which volunteer firemen were loading bodies.

"How many have you got?" McNab called out to one of the firemen. "Seven so far," the fireman responded.

"Any women and children?"

"Babies, all right. Over here." The fireman pointed.

There, piled into a corner, lay Moira and the two infants. They looked like broken dolls, with their limbs akimbo, their skin rubbery and too white. "They yours?" the fireman inquired of McNab. He shook his head and pointed to Digory. "Are they yours, then?" the fireman repeated, this time to Digory, who nodded, unable to speak for choking back a sob. "Didn't know what hit them, fellow," the fireman explained softly. Then he shook his head and spat off to one side, into the churning water. "Woman who owns the house remembered they were down there only when it was too late. Too busy worrying about getting her furniture to higher ground." He reached out from the barge and patted Digory awkwardly on the back — by now, Digory was blubbering. "Anyway, buddy, we got to get them up to Buckovetsky's stockroom. Temporary morgue. They're not the only ones. There'll be more before we're through."

"Come on," McNab urged him. "No point standing here in all this water. Not doing anybody any good. Let these men do their job." He led Digory back up onto dry land, where the Cornishman collapsed in a heap on the ground. "Get up now, man. Get up," the Scot chided. "No point in carrying on this way. God's will, you know."

"No! No! You don't understand," Digory sobbed. "God had nothing to do with it. I killed them. They died because of me."

"They drowned in the flood, man. You had nothing to do with it!" McNab attempted to reason with him.

"No! No!" Digory insisted. "It's all my fault. I thought an ocean was far enough, but I was wrong — *wrong!* — and now they're dead, just like the others!" Glancing up, he spotted Père Henri standing at the top of the street, a small, dark figure clothed in swirling rain. He was overcome with another attack of vertigo. His stomach heaved and his head spun. "Oooh!" he moaned and ducked his head between his knees.

"Enough of that. Come on. On your feet," McNab said. "I tell you what. We'll got to the Moneta. Get you a nice whisky. On the house." He dragged Digory to his feet. "There we go. Come along, now. Why it's Père Henri! Hello, Henri. We were just going back to the Moneta. Our friend here . . ." McNab lowered his voice. "Well, he's had some very bad news."

"Very!" Digory corroborated thickly. He tried to look at the ex-priest, but it was impossible. First he loomed in his vision, then he shrunk, then he guttered like a candle.

"I'm sorry to hear that," the high-grader said.

"You are?" Digory whispered, clinging to McNab.

"Of course," replied the ex-priest.

"My whole family," Digory choked out the words. "Dead! Wiped out!"

"A tragedy," Père Henri agreed. "Well" — and he patted Digory on the shoulder — "perhaps there's a lesson in all this."

"Coming, Henri?" McNab asked.

"Thank you, no. Not tonight. I've done enough work for one day," Père Henri demurred, and turning on his heel, the diminutive Frenchman headed off down the street towards the east. That was the last anyone ever saw of Père Henri. He told no one where he was going; he simply disappeared. When anyone spoke of it, McNab, who, with his slight acquaintance, had known the high-grader better than anyone else, would shrug and say, "Probably went back to where he came from. Wherever that was." As for Digory Pulglase, he never remarried. He lived in the Old Boston Hotel, sharing a sagging bed with a succession of verminous miners, until one May afternoon, nearly sixteen years to the day when he and his father had struck their fateful deal with the bockles, he bit his drill into the side of a drift, hit a bootleg hole and the rock exploded, killing him instantly, as well as the four men working alongside him.